THE ENCORE

A Transformational Thriller

Lauren Holmes

Published by Frontiering
www.frontiering.com
www.laurenholmes.com

To all aspiring worldbuilders

Contents

1

THE TRIP

I don't remember dying thought Connor Kane as he hurtled through an ethereal tunnel. Towards what, he wondered. God? Heaven? The promised light that was to bathe him in feelings of overwhelming peace and love? Unfortunately, I feel only nausea, vertigo, and an overwhelming fear of the unknown. Did these foretell a less desirable destination?

The ragged walls of the tunnel whizzed past him at dizzying speeds. But worse, Connor was ricocheting off the walls upside down, sideways, right side up, then upside down again as if there was no grounding gravity. His aching body felt as if he was being pummeled by a prize fighter.

But wait. He suddenly realized he wasn't colliding with the walls of the tunnel. Rather he was hitting a spongy clear membrane of some sort surrounding him. I'm inside a transparent bubble he concluded as he bounced off the right wall then face-planted into the opposite wall.

He had read about near-death experiences. NDEs. People who had been pronounced clinically dead but been revived. There were no bubbles in their accounts. What did this mean? Their accounts talked about going to the light. There was no bright light ahead of him. Only darkness. Could he not be going to the light? Why was his experience abnormal?

How'd I get here? He searched his memory as he negotiated the collisions. He was still in his tuxedo. He remembered being at the gala celebrating his decade of accomplishments. Then what? Think. He remembered he and Lenore leaving in the limo. Then blackness.

Lenore. Where is she? Panic gripped his body. Is she alright? If I'm dead, she'll be devastated. His heart was besieged with pain at the very thought of her pain. They'd not been apart since their childhood years in the orphanage in Denmark. His heart broke in empathy with the anguish she must be feeling. A second later it hit him that *he'd* no longer be with *her*. His own anguish echoed hers.

Suddenly, the bubble came to a complete stop. His stomach flip-flopped as it does on the downhill drop of a giant roller coaster. The rushing walls of the tunnel were finally still. Silence. Darkness. What is happening? Again, where was the bright light, the beings of light, the welcome of deceased family and friends? Where was his unconditional love and acceptance?

Suddenly, the blue glow of another tunnel materialized out of the pitch black to his right. His bubble immediately made a right turn and raced through the adjoining tunnel. He was again bouncing off the membrane in every direction. He was dizzy again as he was flung from wall to wall upside down.

How can this be? What's going on? Still no bright light up ahead as he was thrust around the endless winding curves characteristic of this second tunnel. Great. Something to make his nausea worse.

Epiphany. I might be able to turn myself right-side up as I bounce off the walls. He dove towards his feet with his upper body then thrust his feet down underneath him. It worked. He was upright. Well this is better he thought.

Wait a minute. Another epiphany. If I'm not near the walls, I won't be battered about like a badminton bird. He softly pushed off the wall with the form of a professional swimmer. He headed for the center of the bubble. Stillness. The cacophony silenced. Phew! The calm in the center of the storm. Well this is better he repeated with self-congratulatory pride.

Now I have a chance to think. What has happened? What is happening? He struggled to remember as he guardedly surveilled the speeding tunnel terrain swishing past his purview. Connor would've liked to have had the out-of-body experience so many NDEs experienced. Floating above, he could've observed his death and the people around his body discussing what had happened. He might then have more answers as to how and perhaps why his life was cut short.

Suddenly Connor's life review launched. He was "seeing his life flash before his eyes" just as most NDEs report happens after death. Finally. Something expected. Maybe he would receive knowledge about his true essence and the nature of the universe. Throughout his life he had continuously craved such knowledge.

A moment later, Connor realized that this life review had actually started before he died. At the gala celebrating his achievements hours ago. For the best decade of his life, Connor Kane had the honor of serving as the very first Commander-in-Chief for Global Human Resource Maximization. It was his job to mobilize the world's human resources into the service of mankind in a time of extreme crisis for humanity.

This position had been created because so many natural and man-made disasters had threatened the survival of the species and the planet. Everyone's greatest talents had to be conscripted to save both. The problems could not be solved by money or power.

Consequently, the existing power holders were willing to relinquish the stage to those with the talent and creativity to solve those challenges. They were motivated by self-interest. They wanted to survive.

According to the praise and awards he'd received, Connor had apparently excelled at this mission. Unfortunately, all government positions were now limited to 10 years in order to give others an opportunity to contribute their talents and creativity.

A paradox. In producing a talent-celebrating world, Connor had spawned the termination of what he considered his greatest opportunity to use his own talents to the fullest. He would dearly have loved to continue as Commander-in-Chief for the rest of his life. He was too young to retire.

Releasing the world's human resources to their full potential in the service of mankind was meaningful work, of course. However, more than this, there was no greater thrill for Connor than enabling people to do their most gratifying work, make their most significant and meaningful contributions, and receive their greatest intrinsic and material rewards. This is what filled his heart.

Accordingly, he and Lenore had spent their entire careers developing the best techniques for individuals to operate at their maximum to achieve their greatest legacy and rewards. That maximum included increasing the breakthroughs and creative inspirations that could bypass hundreds of steps to achieve goals faster. And better he thought in remembering so many unexpected solutions. They had figured out how to create world changers. World builders.

The mission for the global maximization of the world's talents had allowed them to apply those techniques to catalyze transformation on a massive scale. To transform individuals *en masse*. This was his lifework on the grandest of scales.

Yet, neither he nor Lenore had foreseen the peripheral world benefits that would result when talent and the ability to create the unprecedented became supreme. There was no longer tolerance for the prejudice that interfered with the performance of the world's talent assets.

Every glass ceiling was smashed for the ordinary to achieve the extraordinary in the service of mankind. Blocking those who had something to contribute because of their sex, race, religion, birth, financial wherewithal, education, language, culture and whatever was now verboten. Sanctions could be severe. This dramatically changed how the world operated. There was a dedication to constructing a climate favorable to creative breakthroughs to solve the plethora of world crises.

The economy and power structure changed as well. As talent was cherished, those with it were paid massive amounts of money. With the money came power – power to change how the world was run. Life-threatening wars over geography disappeared. So many of humanity's failings were erased. All-in-all, Connor was pleased with his impact and legacy. His life review was good.

Connor was startled out of his reverie by a second abrupt stop of his bubble's whirlwind rush along the tunnel. A second roller coaster stomach flip-flop from the dramatic deceleration. All was dark and still again. Had he arrived? Was this twilight where he was to spend an eternity?

He recalled the previous stop. This likely means the transfer to another tunnel – one which had not yet appeared just like the last time. No NDEs had reported such occurrences. There was a breach in logic here.

He began to question his assumption that he was dead. If this was not death, what could it be? Before he could delve into that answer, the dull blue glow of another tunnel appeared on his right. Seconds later, Connor's bubble was again shooting through this adjoining tunnel as if it was a bobsled on a downhill icy track.

He was very much in descent. As he careened with each turn, he could catch a glimpse of a brilliant crystalline circle of light off in the distance below him. Finally, he would be embraced by the love and peace so many NDE's described. Or would he?

Connor had another eureka moment. As a lover of all things cinematic, his mind was suddenly flooded with visions of wormholes in the *Star Trek* and *Stargate* television series and movies like Christopher Nolan's *Interstellar*. In fact, I think a theoretical physicist designed the wormhole scenes in *Interstellar* he recalled. Kip Thorne? Thorne ensured scientific fidelity. Then it hit him. Could he be travelling through a wormhole rather than crossing over?

What he'd been seeing could just as easily have been a wormhole. Or could it be that death is just a wormhole trip into another dimension or space-time location? He was a man addictively drawn to the exploration of such deep questions. Today he'd no time for such digressions. "Focus" he demanded through the fog of his still-dizzy brain. What did he know about wormholes to help him deal with his current plight?

If he was in a wormhole, he was still alive. He was going to live. This was cause for celebration indeed. This was the first good thought he'd had on this trip. He might still be alive?

What did he know about wormholes? A wormhole is a conduit through 4-dimensional space-time. Wormholes are considered to bend space and time to allow two vastly separated regions of the universe to connect. He remembered some video from his past in which two points were drawn on a piece of paper and then the paper was folded so that the two points touched. The wormhole connected these two points. Space commutes that might take thousands of years could be achieved in minutes or hours.

There must be a network of wormholes. I wonder if some civilization made such a network or was it a natural phenomenon. They would have to be pretty advanced to achieve such a construction he ruminated. That would explain the pauses. A wormhole into a different direction was required to speed my bubble to its destination.

Darn! I might be light years away from Earth. Wormholes allow interstellar, intergalactic, and sometimes even interuniversal travel within human lifetime scales. They have also served as a method for time travel.

Didn't Stephen Hawking posit that wormholes might theoretically be utilized for travel through time as well as through space? Well, that is disconcerting. I might not only be a great distance from Lenore. I might also be in another time. They would be separated as the lovers on the TV show *Outlander*. Did he accidentally pass through a special Stonehenge-type rock as Caitriona Balfe did in her role as Claire Randall?

What was that thrilling 90s-something movie with Jody Foster? It was a Carl Sagan novel. *Contact.* Jody Foster's Dr. Ellie Arroway travels 26 light years through a series of wormholes to the star Vega. The round trip, which to Ellie lasts 18 hours, passes by in a fraction of a second on Earth, making it appear she went nowhere.

Am I living science fiction or just dreaming it? How long have I been traveling? He had no idea. Gosh, he could be thousands of miles from his home. How was he going to get back? His anxiety was interrupted by suddenly glimpsing the circular brilliant white light again only a few turns away.

To Connor's surprise there was another bubble in front of his. No. There were two! What did that mean? He was not the only one kidnapped? These were his kidnappers? His fear of being battered about again kept him anchored to the center of his bubble.

However, he stretched cautiously off-center to try to see who else had come from Earth. He could not make out who stepped out of the two bubbles. The de-loading seemed to take place in some kind of station structure. How did the bubbles know to come to this station he wondered?

For the first time, Connor noticed circuitry in the base wall of his bubble. It had been in the dark during his trip. Now there was illumination. How ingeniously compact. Since childhood he had always been delighted by creative breakthroughs of every kind. The thrill of helping people to realize creative potential to make their greatest breakthroughs for humanity had always been what had driven his lifework.

His bubble suddenly decelerated for a third time. His stomach did the usual roller-coaster flip-flop. The rushing walls of the tunnel slowed to a snail's pace. The light of the station was getting brighter making it difficult to see through his unaccustomed eyes. He could discern beings on the disembarkation platform but could not identify them as human.

Before he had time to contemplate his pending meeting, Connor found himself floating to the bottom of his bubble as it came to a complete stop. He was now standing on very wobbly legs. No more. He reached to grab the side of the bubble to steady himself. Unsuccessful, he crumpled to the floor in a heap. He was surprised to discover he had no muscles.

The deceleration must've made his fall to the bottom of the bubble possible. No. It must be that he had arrived at a planet with gravitational pull. He wondered where he could be. He wondered whether he would be greeted by friend or foe. He wondered what form they might take. Would they be human? Connor was once more overcome with fear and trepidation.

2

THE ARRIVAL

Connor was still blinded by the bright lights of the station after spending hours in darkness. He couldn't make out his surroundings or their inhabitants. He put up his arm to shield his eyes to give them time to become accustomed. The silence was welcome after hours of the rush of air from accelerated travel.

Before he could regain his senses, a narrow slit opened in the wall of the bubble. Someone or something much larger than himself lifted him off the floor and carried him through this opening. He was placed on a gurney like those used in ambulances. A being in a white coat with the air of a doctor began checking his vitals.

As soon as the doctor was done, the bed was raised under his head so that Connor was sitting up. He found himself staring at a dozen faces. The most benevolent and wise of the beings spoke first.

"Welcome to Annutia, Commander-in-Chief Connor Kane, Global Human Resources Maximization. I'm Minister Plenipotentiary Axl Dahl. I have just been retired from my role as Supreme Commander for the same reasons you were retired. Term. It was I who wished for your presence here. You may address me as Minister for the present."

Minister Plenipotentiary. Strange to have this familiar but remote title. Connor hadn't heard that title since grade school history. In the 1783 Peace Treaty of Versailles which terminated the American Revolution, John Adams, Benjamin Franklin and John Jay were named Minister Plenipotentiary of the United States to the Netherlands, France and Spain, respectively.

Connor analyzed the Minister as he contemplated a response. He was gracious, friendly, and immediately likeable as befits a diplomatic role. However, Connor was not deceived. The power of the Supreme Commander's past authority and leadership was bristling just below the surface. This was a strong achievement-driven man of great depth.

He seemed to sincerely value Connor and treated him almost familially. This was interesting because Axl Dahl was so similar in appearance to Connor that he could've been a relative. Both men had Nordic features. Blue eyes. Light skin and hair. Angular features. They were both tall with wiry athletic builds. The Minister was perhaps 15 years older.

"May I know the purpose of my abduction, Minister?" Connor came directly to the point.

"We need your assistance, Commander."

"I've retired from my post, Minister. Please call me Connor – a planned familiarity in contrast to Axl's formality. How may I help?"

Axl smiled at Connor's bonding maneuver but did not reciprocate. "You're tired now, Connor. Sleep. We'll talk when you awake."

"Annalise! A lithe black-skinned beauty with arresting azure eyes stepped into the spotlight surrounding Connor's gurney. "Could you please deliver Commander Kane to his residence and bring him to me when he's refreshed?"

"Yes, Minister" said Annalise.

With a take-charge manner, she motioned to two guards to push Connor's bed into the awaiting ambulance. Annalise appeared aristocratic, intelligent, capable, and physically and emotionally powerful beneath a diplomatic demeanor. Her large expressive eyes were electric. Even otherworldly. Yet they revealed a depth that made her worthy of a former Supreme Commander's trust. Consequently, Connor felt he could trust her as well.

It was unusual to see such a muscular physique on such a lean female frame. She was tall. Perhaps equal to his own 6 feet. Maybe a few inches less. Annalise made efficient use of the time as he was transported to the residence.

"Welcome, Commander Kane. We're delighted to have you with us. I'm one of many who have admired the unprecedented revolution you inspired and implemented on planet Earth over the last 10 years.

"It will be my job to provide you with all of the resources that you'll need to accomplish the same goals here in a much shorter timeframe. I'm charged with educating you about our world. I am also responsible for your safety and your interface with the members of the Annutia Planetary Steering Council. I hope I'll become a trusted advisor and confidant for your mission, Commander.

"My talents, training, education, and passions all favor such a role. I too am committed to each person achieving their greatest lifetime legacy in the service of Annutia's civilization." She talked on enthusiastically in this vein for some time about their common interests and goals. Connor recognized that this was an attempt to distract him from his plight. He knew in that moment that Annalise had a good heart.

Within about ten minutes they'd arrived at a luxury apartment on a very high floor. Annalise opened the door. "This will be your residence, Commander. These guards will carry you in as your ability to walk will likely still be compromised. One of them will always remain outside your door to ensure you are safe and in case you need anything. This is Brik. And this is Jon. Gentlemen, if you will."

She stepped into the lavish suite and held open the door. Brik and Jon carried Connor to the master bedroom and placed him on the king-sized bed. A lush royal blue robe had been laid out for him on the turned-down bed. There were also silk pajamas in the same blue and a high-end black hoodie with matching sweatpants from which to choose.

"If you'll change, Commander, we'll see to the cleaning of your tuxedo and other garments and shoes, so they're ready when you want them. Additional clothes, shoes, and accessories have been placed in the closets and drawers for your use.

"Please let us know whatever else you need, Commander Kane. Just press the intercom button and Service will answer. Press 8 if you need to talk to me directly. If there's an emergency, key 911. They'll know who and where you are. We created it just for you based on its familiar usage on Earth.

"Do you know what kind of food you'd like to eat right now, Commander? What kind of food and drink you'd like in your fridge? What you'd want to eat when you wake up? I've taken the liberty of keeping warm our version of a hamburger and fries in the oven and a strawberry milkshake in the fridge. Would they do for now?"

"Very much, thank you," replied Connor. I hadn't realized how hungry I am."

"Jon, if you wouldn't mind." She motioned him to the kitchen. "I have bacon, eggs, rolls, and fruit in the fridge for breakfast or you may order from room service over the intercom. There are checklists for prepared foods and grocery items on the nightstand, so you can select what will keep you fueled for your mission. There's also a third checklist for any nonfood items you might need. Just leave the lists on the kitchen counter. Housekeeping will collect them daily.

"We've already provided a computer, printer, and other technology you may require. The remote for this television is in your night stand. I've stocked the bookshelves with books about Annutia and Annutians, so please feel free to browse to learn more about the people you're here to help. There is gym equipment in a room off the living room in case you need to work out.

"Press 8 when you're ready for me to return to escort you to meet with the Minister Plenipotentiary. Is there anything else you require, Commander?"

"When will I be going home, Annalise?" When she did not respond, Connor asked, "Can I contact my wife to let her know that I'm alright? We've never been separated. She must be terrified." Again, Annalise seemed to have difficulty finding the words to respond.

"Do I have any choice in whether I take on this mission?"

"Hm," responded Annalise with immediate understanding and empathy. "Perhaps these are questions best put to the Minister. Unfortunately, there are matters for which I haven't been authorized to speak, Commander. I'll be as open as I can throughout our partnership.

"However, if I can't provide you with the information you request, I'll refrain from saying anything rather than lie to you. I want you to feel you can trust what I do say. Good night, sir," she said as she moved swiftly towards the door of the bedroom. She obviously wanted no part in contributing to his pain.

"Good night, Annalise. Thank you," he called after her to let her know he understood and did not hold her responsible.

Connor dove into his food wholeheartedly, appreciative of the Annutians' attempt to provide him with a favorite American meal. I wonder if they have a MacDonald's here yet? He smiled as he envisaged himself negotiating that lucrative trade deal if they didn't. And Jeff Bezos would certainly want to launch Amazon here – likely in person given his love of space travel and science fiction. And that is exactly what this was thought Connor. Science fiction.

3
THE MISSION

Connor pressed 8 on his intercom to summon Annalise for his rendezvous with Minister Plenipotentiary Axl Dahl. He was rested, showered, dressed, and nourished. He was ready to negotiate with the Minister for a few things, especially the terms of his return home. Annalise arrived to collect him. She nodded towards the elevator when she caught Brik's eye as they passed him seated at the guard table outside of Connor's door. He followed behind.

As the trio descended in the elevator of the residential tower, Annalise explained that six planetary government towers were connected at ground level and one floor below via shopping and restaurant concourses. When they reached the ground level, Connor was impressed with the massiveness of the complex and the elegance of the stores and restaurants.

In places, ceilings were several floors high to create an impressive spaciousness. Several floors of people-filled glassed-in offices overlooked the concourse. The complex was stone, glass, and steel in an uplifting blue and white theme. It looked like a mixture of blue marble, blue granite, white marble and white granite with the granite being used for the floors.

Rather than a cold impersonal isolating structure, this hub was alive with people of purpose from many races. We have no such planetary capital on Earth he thought. But if we did, I imagine it would look like this.

The trio walked over to the elevator for Tower West and sped up to floor 68 at the top of the tower. The elevators had glass walls as well. Even though he didn't think he had a fear of heights, Connor found it unnerving to be exposed to the view from such a height. He'd had a visceral reaction to the speed of the elevator rise. He suspected that he was still sensitive from the trauma of his recent wormhole voyage.

As he and Annalise entered the Minister's spacious office foyer, it was obvious that there was some pressing crisis afoot. Axl's Aides were white with fear as they stood around the Minister's desk in his inner office. They were intent on expressing their concerns, demanding solutions, and asking questions as he listened paternally. He eventually stopped them by suddenly standing up to begin issuing orders to each. The Aides quickly dispersed, somewhat relieved to have assignments to address their issues.

"Would you like to reschedule your meeting with Commander Kane, Minister?" asked a respectful Annalise.

"No. No. Good morning, Annalise, Commander," he said with a nod to each. "Commander, please come in," he welcomed. "Make yourself comfortable," he said as he waved Connor to a large grouping of rounded deep tufted leather couches and stately wing-back chairs. "Coffee, expresso, latte, macchiato, iced latte, juice," Axl offered from an elaborate built-in bar laden with refreshments and associated machines and carafes. He opened a full-sized fridge hidden behind the wall of wood paneling to reveal a large assortment of cold beverages and snacks.

"A Latte, please."

"Allow me, Minister."

"Thank you, Annalise."

The Minister took a large chair across from Connor and scrutinized him for a moment. Connor, for his part was engrossed with the massiveness of the office. He'd been in the offices of many national leaders across Earth. Yet he'd never been in one so large or lavish.

One end of the office was completely windows. The view was spectacular from the 68th floor. The windows extended inwards along the ceiling for about five feet making it appear from his seat that the office was suspended in the sky. It functioned much like an upside-down infinity pool with no boundary to the sky. This was architecturally foreign to anything Connor had encountered on Earth.

As Annalise presented the latte to Connor, she went to sit down adjacent to him. "Thank you, Annalise. I need to speak to the Commander alone. Please let Birgitte know where we might contact you when Commander Kane is ready to return to his residence."

"Of course, Minister," she said good-naturedly as she glided gracefully across the office towards the door. If she was disappointed at being excluded, her face did not divulge it. He admired Annalise as a natural diplomat. She had such a pleasant uplifting energy. Conner's mind immediately switched back to business. He took charge of the meeting.

"I'll need to speak to my wife before we continue. I need to tell her that I'm alright and how long it'll be before I come home."

The Minister darted a glance at the departing Annalise.

"Annalise, please arrange a call for Connor so he may calm his wife."

For a second, a quizzical look passed across her face before she composed herself.

Connor worried what that was about. Given Annalise's normal state of composure her momentary lapse was even more significant.

"Will two hours from now be enough time, Minister?"

"Very good, Annalise."

She closed the door.

The Minister adroitly snatched the agenda back from Connor. He was obviously a man accustomed to running things.

"Connor, our circumstances are dire."

Connor noted that now that they were behind closed doors without an audience, Axl had dropped the decorum and deference of addressing him by his title. The Minister had accepted his previous invitation for a less formal relationship.

"If creative solutions are not found, an alien transmutation of this planet will make it uninhabitable by human beings. We have perhaps only six months to live. What I will tell you now is known only by those who have signed confidentiality agreements. You'll be addressing twelve of these tomorrow morning at a meeting of the Annutia Planetary Steering Council.

"I will respect your wishes for confidentiality, Axl," assured Connor. Am I going to like this *cultural transformation project* for which you've *volunteered* me?" he asked facetiously with a teasing grin.

In reality, Connor was seething inside now that he knew he had not just been kidnapped but was also facing imminent death on a dying planet. With the practiced discipline of decades, there was not a ripple of his anger, fear, or weakness anywhere on his face. Provocation while powerlessly imprisoned on a foreign planet would not be the smartest strategy. His platform for negotiation would dissipate.

"We are requesting an encore, Connor, of your greatest work. If I've read you correctly, I'm confident that there's nothing you'd rather do. Do you understand the term 'terraforming'?"

"Yes," grinned Connor. I confess that I enjoy the worldbuilding dilemmas of many science fiction novels. Terraforming or literally, 'Earth-shaping', is a process for modifying planets, moons, asteroids and such to make them habitable by Earth-like life, especially humans.

"Good. Our scientists have found evidence that Annutia was originally terraformed – probably by people traveling from Earth through the wormhole long before vehicles for space travel were developed. Now some alien species is trying to change the planet back. Or at least trying to customize it to their needs. We're not sure yet."

"We don't yet have a word for this planetary engineering to a non-Earth-friendly ecology. So, for convenience I borrowed the term 'xenoforming' from

H.G. Wells in his 1898 novel, *The War of the Worlds* – the re-engineering of Earth or an Earth-like planet to benefit some alien population. 'Xeno' pertains to foreign or foreigner."

Axl abruptly stood up in the middle of the discussion and walked to the coffee bar. While he presented a calm and in-control exterior, it was obviously a façade constructed with a discipline similar to Connor's. He asked Connor if he too would like another. Connor asked for sparkling mineral water. Ice. Lemon. The Minister returned and continued with some urgency.

"There are other wormholes near Annutia from which the aliens must have arrived. We have no flying machines. They were banned when the factions kept bombing each other or hijacking planes for ransom or using them for kamikaze missions. Therefore, we'd have noticed any encroachment by air. With the kind of stealth used, there was no way for us to know to protect ourselves. We have weapons against invaders, of course, but this attack was too low key to be detected.

Rather, the aliens, whomever they are, patiently infected the planet with a deadly cocktail of algae which our scientists predict will gradually convert our atmosphere to their preference. Oxygen will be eliminated. An ample supply of ammonia, nitrates, and phosphates were apparently included in the cocktail to ensure that the algae flourished and spread rapidly. Before this, algae were unknown on this planet."

Axl abruptly stood up again to address a mounted super-sized map of the planet on Connor's behalf. It covered most of the wall opposite the window. Lighting of various areas or categories was controlled by a board of buttons at the bottom. Axl hit a button and some bodies of water were highlighted in red.

"The fatal effects of the xenoforming cocktail are spreading rapidly. The algae emit gases and neurotoxins that are deadly to human beings and indeed all living things plant and animal. These areas in red here, here, here, here, and here are particularly noxious. The old and sick in these red zones are beginning to register respiratory distress.

"Apparently, algal toxins can be aerosolized by water waves. Airborne algal toxins trigger allergy- and asthma-like symptoms such as airway constriction, shortness of breath, sneezing, and so on. Persons with preexisting airway disease are most affected. The toxins are released as the algae die and begin to decompose.

"The algae grow wherever there is moisture and particularly where they've been supplied with significant sources of phosphorus, nitrogen, and carbon. Accordingly, the algae gravitate to our lakes and rivers and are contaminating our water with neurotoxins and such," he said as he returned to his seat with a laser pointer and a remote. "Even water intrusion into buildings that are not immediately addressed tend to support the growth of the poisonous algae making our buildings unsafe or uninhabitable.

"We're already facing water shortages. Our existing water filtration systems are ill-equipped to handle the current levels of contamination. Our water treatment systems can no longer screen out the concentrations of deadly neurotoxins in the water.

"In addition, the whole food chain has been affected. The neurotoxins have accumulated in the bodies of shellfish, sardines, and anchovies, which, if then eaten by sea lions, otters, cetaceans, birds or people, can cause death. The algae cover the water and prevent the sunlight required by plants living below from reaching them. Animals dependent on those plants are then starved out.

"We assume these algae are food for the aliens. Our think tanks have explored the idea that the invaders will allow our population to suffocate due to respiratory challenges and/or to die from dehydration or starvation. They can then simply assume possession of Annutia when we're all dead. By then, they'll have the sustainable food supply and atmosphere that they need.

"Our brainstorming groups have also contemplated the scenario in which Annutians could be enslaved by the aliens based on our need for oxygen, water, and food. Therefore, they might invade when some of us are still living.

"The crisis you observed upon your arrival today, Connor, was the outbreak of a fire. Some of the farmers along our main waterway here" as he pointed the laser light to the largest river, "tried to kill the algae by burning them.

"There were unexpected flammable gases that didn't burn the algae at all. The fire simply existed above the algae blooms. Much like the effect of fire eaters and fire tracers who protect themselves with 70% isopropyl alcohol, white gas, naphtha fuel, or stunt fire gel on their skin as insulation. The invaders must have planned for our use of fire as a defense as well.

"Our food chains have been affected. Our fish industry is dead. Our meat industry is quickly disappearing as the animal sources are dying from the toxicity from infected water, feed, and the food chain. Our water is gone. The laser light darted back to the map to follow the outline of the same largest and longest river. We also get hydropower from the flow of the Kalix River which has been blocked by the algae.

"The farms that have grown up along our Kalix River because of the need for fresh water, no longer have access to it. Toxic water has killed both cattle and crops. We're facing a severe food shortage as a result.

"The factions, tribes, and castes with water are demanding payment for what was previously shared. They have been stockpiling resources for the starving, thirsty populations in their own jurisdictions.

"We're having to increase our use of fossil fuels such as coal and oil for power. There's a corresponding increase in carbon dioxide emissions which are affecting the ozone layer to make our environmental problems worse.

"Coal-fired power plants spew billions of tons of climate-changing CO2 into the atmosphere which causes a greenhouse effect. Greenhouse gases trap the heat from the sun causing global warming. The most common heat-trapping gases are water vapor, carbon dioxide, methane, and ozone. The resulting global warming causes . . . ."

The intensity of the discussion was suddenly interrupted by a sharp knock at the door. A well-dressed gentleman burst into the office at a speed which prevented Axl from diplomatically rebuffing him. He immediately headed to Connor with an outstretched hand.

"Welcome. I'm Supreme Commander Rikard Riis," he said bombastically.

With a respondent handshake, Connor replied at normal conversational decibels, "Connor Kane, former Commander-in-Chief, Global Human Resources Maximization, Earth. A pleasure to meet you, Supreme Commander."

"Please call me Rikard, Connor. You are a most welcome addition to our life-and-death fight. Thank you for agreeing to help us. I look forward to hearing you introduce your process tomorrow at the Council meeting. My wife Ingrid and I would be delighted if you'd join us for dinner in the next few days as your schedule permits."

"Thank you, Rikard. I'd be delighted," responded Connor perfunctorily.

"Pardon my intrusion, Axl," he said finally acknowledging the Minister's presence with a nod in his direction. "I'll leave you gentlemen to your important work." With that, Rikard turned and abruptly exited the office with the same speed at which he had burst into it.

Supreme Commander Riis has the charm, charisma and sociability of successful politicians. However, he has very little of the substance that Axl possesses. It was obvious to Connor that someone had bought this man's way into his current position. Riis was a front. A puppet. And by the strain he sensed between the two men, Connor suspected that Axl was not the puppet master but the enemy.

Riis also lacked Axl's benevolence. In fact, there was a foreboding in his manner which made Connor fearful. He realized that he would be even more uneasy if Axl was no longer there to protect him. In an instant, he realized his dependence on the Minister. He accepted that Axl was friend not foe.

Alone again, Connor restarted the discussion, "So have you brought me here to die, Axl? I fear our friendship is going to be short-lived," he quipped.

Axl laughed. "I must have more faith in you than you do, Connor."

Connor continued to jest to break Axl's tension. He motioned to the large picture on the wall of Vaudeville comedy duo and silent film comedians, Stan Laurel and Oliver Hardy. Their famous catch phrase was printed boldly on the top, "Well, here's another nice mess you've gotten me into!"

"I relate, Axl. I suspect I'm not the first," he joked.

Axl laughed again succumbing to the distraction. "Would you believe this is the oldest known relic from Earth? I 've often wondered if it suggests the time when Annutia was terraformed. Laurel and Hardy were famous from the late 1920s to the 1940s. Annutians tend not to concentrate on history as much as they do on Earth because our religion has us focusing on the 'now.' We're taught mindfulness and contemplative techniques and practices in school from the first grade to help us to do that.

"Obviously, we need creative solutions now, Connor. We need you to repeat with acceleration your conversion of humanity to a talent- and creativity-worshipping power structure. We need our world's talents working at the maximum to save our planet and ourselves. There is no one better than you to do that."

"Thank you, sir."

"Unfortunately, we're a population devoid of creativity. We have so many rules, and so many castes and so much prejudice and judgement that we've all but eliminated the courage to be creative. We've become a left-brain society where logic reigns supreme. Our creative right brains have atrophied.

"What makes you think there is enough time, Axl?"

"I've studied your career, Connor. You've worked on the liberation of individuals to their full creative expression for 30 years. When you assumed the role of Commander-in-Chief for Global Human Resources Maximization, you had your strategic plan completed and being actioned in your first month. You established most of the structures for global conversion in your first two months. What is it you call yourself? Oh yes. *An execution creative.*

"This is your encore, Connor. Faster. Smarter. With higher stakes. And with more fulfillment than the first time around. There is no project more meaningful for you to undertake.

"If you went back to your retirement on Earth without at least trying, you'd regret it for the rest of your life. Facing death is not the anathema for you, Commander Kane. Facing a life without meaning, purpose, and mission is far worse for someone of your talents and passions.

"You'll see, Connor. We've already started. We've released your speeches and writings into our corporations and upper educational streams to get people thinking about the conversion.

"I'm going to have Annalise arrange for you to access to the Planetary Government Library today. You'll get an idea of how much we know already so you can formulate what you want to say to the Council tomorrow about your plan."

Connor refrained from comment while he began to formulate possible strategies. He was indeed an execution creative by passion. He believed he could implement anything even if it had never been done before. He found new implementation challenges irresistible.

"I've studied your methods for achieving the restructuring to release the greatest creative solutions to global crises. However, what I haven't been able to figure out yet is what levers you pushed to cause the break in the money-and-political power grid in the first place. A discussion for another day."

Connor suspected Axl was referencing the forces behind Rikard Riis. The Minister jumped up without warning for a third time and stepped quickly to his desk to flick on the intercom. "Birgitte, has Annalise returned yet for Commander Kane?"

"Yes, sir. She's been here for some time."

Axl moved to the door and opened it.

"So sorry to have kept you, Annalise. Please come in for a moment. Commander Kane needs library access to Earth information to find common ground for his speech to the Council tomorrow. He's also going to need information about the Council Ministers, so he can shape his speech to his audience.

"I think it's also advisable that you make him aware of the conflicts among them so that he's not blindsided. In fact, why don't you bring him at the beginning of the Council meeting so that he can observe the conflicts and players in action.

"Thank you, Annalise. And thank you Commander Kane for undertaking this critical mission for us," Axl said while shaking Connor's hand. "I look forward to hearing you speak. Please use Annalise to let me know how I may help."

And without even a moment to consider or to ask a question, Connor suddenly found himself outside of the Minister's inner office next to its closed door. Connor was impressed by how smooth Axl was. He felt out-finessed.

"This way, Commander," directed Annalise. The tall and muscled Brik again trailed them. Obviously, Axl considered him a VIP needing a bodyguard.

"Were you able to arrange the call with my wife?"

"I was indeed. We have thirty minutes to arrive back at the appointed time."

As they stepped out of the elevator on his floor of the residential tower, Connor could see at the other end of the hall Jon sitting at the table guarding his suite. Perhaps Axl was right. Maybe he'd underestimated his talents somewhat despite the celebratory gala.

As they arrived at the suite, Annalise walked to the office where an external telephone resided. Connor took the covers off his lunch while he pondered how he was going to tell Lenore that there was a good chance that he would be dead within the year.

4

LENORE'S CALL

Connor sat eating his lunch at the kitchen counter. Or at least pushing his food around the plate. He was too nervous about talking to Lenore to eat. What could he say on the call to put her mind at ease? She would see right through any attempt to comfort her. She could always tell if he was lying or lying by omission.

Since they were small children, they'd always known what each other was thinking. They had continually finished each other's sentences. They immediately felt what the other felt whether together or miles apart.

How was he going to keep her from knowing that his life was at risk? That he was likely going to die within the next year. That he had been kidnapped. That he was being held prisoner. That he would never see her again. That despite all of that, he was about to undertake the most exciting work of his life.

How did Axl know him so well? There was a bond there. Almost familial. Perhaps he could tell Lenore about that and the work to distract her from the things he wanted to hide. There. That was the strategy he was seeking.

He was still too nervous to eat. His expensive gourmet meal was going to go to waste. Brik, the meat eater, will so enjoy it, he thought. He opened the door to invite him in. To his surprise there was a stranger there.

"Is there something I can get for you, sir? "

"Where is Brik?"

"He has been called away, Commander. My name is Niels. Brik will be back in a few minutes."

"Where is Jon?"

"He's sleeping to be ready for the next shift."

"Would you like my food, Niels? It's just going to go to waste."

"Thank you, sir. Unfortunately, they have zero tolerance for us to be distracted from protecting you."

"Would you like my food, Niels?"

"Absolutely, sir. Thank you," Niels said with a laugh.

Annalise popped her head out of the office. "It's time for your call, Commander."

"Thank you, Annalise," Connor said as he entered the office. "Do I look alright?" he joked nervously smoothing his hair and eyebrows.

Annalise laughed as she vacated the room and closed the door behind herself.

"Hello?"

"Connie, my love, are you alright?"

Connor was immediately on his guard. Why would she call him Connie? He had staged a revolt at the orphanage on his fifth birthday. He refused to respond to anyone who called him Connie. He was too old to be called Connie. And anyway, it was a girl's name. What was she trying to convey?

"I love you, Lenore. I miss you. I'm so sorry I couldn't call before now. I'm alright."

"I love you, Connie. I was terrified. I'm so much better now just to hear your voice."

"I'm going to continue our mission, my love. It's important work. Perhaps the most important I've ever done. It's extremely confidential. It may take me a few months to complete. I have a good boss who seems to know both me and my work well. I wish you were here to work by my side."

"You *know* I'm always with you in your heart, Connie. And when I look at the remoteness of your favorite view from home, you'll always be with me. Not time nor space can separate us. I'm . . ."

Connor heard noises on the line that suggested disconnection.

"Lenore? Are you still there?" The line was silent. Not even a dial tone. That was strange.

And so was her calling him Connie. She was trying to communicate a message in code. What was it? And why did she need to speak in code at all?

Was she a prisoner as well? Were they holding her hostage at their home in case he didn't cooperate? The very thought of it struck him to his core. He was helpless to protect her. What remote view was she talking about? What was she trying to tell him?

Annalise knocked on the door.

"Enter," he called.

"If you'll turn on the computer on your desk, I'll bring up the Earth and Annutia research from the Planetary Government Library which may inform your speech preparation for tomorrow." She sat down in a big easy chair and began keying into a laptop. Connor escaped into the work at hand to avoid his fears.

5

CONNOR'S COUNCIL SPEECH

Connor and Annalise quietly let themselves into the elaborate Council Chamber where the Annutia Planetary Steering Council meeting was underway. They took seats in the audience amphitheater high at the back where it was dimly lit. There was no one else in the audience. The twelve Ministers seated around the brightly lit oval conference table were too deeply embroiled in debate to notice their entrance. This included Axl Dahl and Rikard Riis seated appropriately at opposite ends of the long, luxurious table.

The current argument was over water rights as Axl had forewarned. The algae cocktail had drastically reduced available water. The filtration systems were inadequate to the challenge of clearing out the toxins. The delegates with water made it clear that as clean water became scarce it was no longer going to be shared with the factions without water despite agreements to the contrary being in place. As Axl had suggested, Connor took note of the positions and conflicts to better understand his audience.

From his research, Connor recognized the water-rich Varunian leader and the water-poor KahlDahr leader at the center of the conflict. It was decided that the Varunians had to honor the water contracts or all other contracts would be deemed invalid.

Economic sanctions meant that trade with the Varunians would be boycotted. No defense or security contracts would be honored for the Varunians. No fire or medical services reinforcements. This really hit home given the repercussions of the spread of today's algae fire started by the farmers along the Kalix River. And the list went on.

Not surprisingly, the Varunians eventually capitulated and decided that they would continue to share their water. The Chief of State of the Azurites graciously offered to share their much stronger and more advanced water filtration systems. The filters of the other factions were failing with the increased load of the alien cocktail. Additional compensation for the Azurites' generosity was ratified by all parties.

These were Annalise's people. The Azurites were named for their electric blue eyes. Yet, their black skin appeared to be a much more defining feature. They were represented by Chief of State Einar Nyhus. He was decidedly impressive with his generosity of spirit and gracious congeniality. Nyhus had a demeanor similar to that of Annalise: poised, articulate, professional, diplomatic, and intelligent. Connor suspected they were friends.

"Commander Kane," called Axl as he waved him forward.

Connor was shaken out of his musings. As he rose to move towards the bright lights of the table, he noticed all twelve Council members quickly scanning the tablets in front of them. He suspected that he'd already been introduced to them in detail.

"Everyone here has been briefed, Commander," confirmed Axl as he slid his chair from the head of the table to the side. "You have the floor," he said motioning Connor to replace him.

Connor stood at the head of the table collecting his thoughts on what he wanted to say. Suddenly his thoughts were arrested by the sheer beauty of the high-gloss, deeply burled wood of the long thick tabletop. He had never seen anything like it on Earth. The three-dimensional complexity and convolutions of the pronounced grain patterns pulled him into their depths, grounding him.

It incited within him a resonance upon which he had come to rely to signal that he was taking the right path. In an instant, everything he was about to say was recolored with new meaning and purpose. It was infused with new energy and inspiration. He was transformed from coerced to committed. He began his speech from a new depth.

"The simultaneous occurrence of a number of crises which threatened the survival of Earth and humanity fueled a dramatic change in the power structure which had dominated our planet. Those with the greatest power and/or money came to realize that all the power and money in the world were not going to save them. They had no choice but to relinquish the reins to 'lesser beings' more creative and talented than they were who could solve the problems.

"The creativity and inventiveness of the world's human resources were unleashed to find solutions. Brilliant breakthroughs defeated the crises. Humanity survived. Civilization evolved into a more advanced level of existence.

"I'd been recruited as Commander-in-Chief, Global Human Resources Maximization because I'd had unusual success over a few decades in creating world changers. Worldbuilders, may be more precise. The key to my methods was a dedication to the daily use and improvement of one's strongest most rewarding talents. This was our maximum. Our peak performance.

"I discovered that, once engaged, we had evolved mechanisms to addict us to operating at this maximum as you would expect of any successful species. My formula triggered these addictive survival mechanisms for maximization. Magic happened as a result of living this maximum day after day.

"An overdrive state emerged which exceeded known human potential. It was a state of genius which we routinely observe in savants who do not have the brain capacity to express such genius. It was the state of spontaneous knowledge which those who've had near death events universally describe.

"What emerged from my formula was serial breakthroughs, flashes of genius, creative inspirations, and other forms of spontaneous knowledge. Whole systems or 'books' of relevant information seem to download into their heads to help them complete the task at hand. One breakthrough could bypass hundreds of steps necessary to achieving a goal.

"The internal mechanisms humans had evolved to pressure peak performance to improve our chances of survival include addictive drives, biochemistry, positive emotions and passions, to name a few.

"These mechanisms are part of the same system we have evolved to maximize the health of our bodies. But our pressure to maximize appears to be larger than an internal maximizing process.

"It became evident that human beings are linked to a larger external maximization process with which they have co-evolved. This external maximizing machinery seeks to maximize all living things synergistically, symbiotically, and synchronously.

"This extension of our internal resources with external resources was the source of the overdrive state I discovered. It was a new level of peak performance and human potential. The formula I invented was the means to invoke this overdrive state.

"Recruiting this external maximization machinery occurs automatically when one is operating at one's maximum. This is because maximization internally and externally is a single system. We have not evolved to operate as separate entities. When one is complying with the direction of one's maximizing machinery internally, one will automatically merge with the external maximizing machinery.

"Because this machinery is advancing all living systems, I call it *the bioflow*. It is the direction of the co-evolution of all living species. When we comply with the bioflow, our capabilities are suddenly extended by the power, information, direction, synergy, and evolution of all living systems. We can achieve beyond our internal potential.

"To complete my overdrive formula, I discovered a fast route to maximization. A built-in mechanism that humanity has evolved. I discovered *savantflow*. We've all experienced ordinary flow states. They are periods of altered consciousness that arise from hyperfocus on an activity.

"They are sessions of complete absorption in an activity such that time, place, and sense of self disappear. They invoke activity fusion, if you will. Normally, our brains fire chaotically. However, in flow, one's entire brain unifies to a cohesive focus on the activity at hand. Peak performance results."

"Are you talking about that 1990 book called *Flow: The Psychology of Optimal Experience* by a name I can't pronounce?" asked Nyhus as he looked up from his tablet.

"Csikszentmihalyi (cheek-sent-me-high-ee)," responded Connor. "And yes, this is the generic peak performance flow state to which I'm referring.

"Savantflow is a specialized subset which I identified. It occurs when the flow state experienced arises specifically from applying one's strongest most rewarding talents and strengths in the most meaningful way for the most appreciative or valuing audience.

"This is the formula for the true maximum performance of anyone's system. Savantflow is the way for us to automatically flick into maximized state."

Grand General Haugstad, the head of armed forces, interjected, "Did physicist David Bohm not talk about a 'holomovement.' How does this fit with the bioflow you're describing?"

"For simplicity, you can assume they are one and the same, Grand General Haugstad. You can assume a singular integrated, synergistic, and synchronous flow or pulsation for all successful living systems. Every successful living system is co-evolving dynamically." Haugstad nodded.

"This organizing bioflow continuously puts each living system into proximity with the information they need to advance and maximize," continued Connor. "Think of every living system as simply an information system.

"Think of nature as a librarian who organizes these living information systems to the advantage of the majority and priority. When one merges with the larger maximization machinery, the librarian will position you advantageously in the database to source the information you need next for the task you're focused on in your savantflow. The information you need for your continued or sustained maximization."

"You said 'goals which will maximize them,'" interrupted KahlDahr Chief of State Lennart Lorenson. "So then not every goal will be supported by the bioflow?"

"Correct, Minister Lorenson. And an astute observation. One must frame one's goal in the direction of the internal-external maximizing process if one wants the bioflow to accelerate and enhance its achievement. *Each of us can know what future goals will be supported based on what goals were supported in our past.*

"One's maximum is a constant. The way the bioflow pressures your system to maximize is a constant. Therefore, what was supported in your past will be supported in your future. You will know which projects will succeed or fail based on your history. *You'll have predictability.*

"If you're trying to obtain money to perpetuate a state of sub-maximization, or worse, a detrimental state, you'll have to fight upstream against a bioflow intent on maximizing you," explained Connor.

"Would the corollary be supported?" asked Rikard Riis. Connor had to smile to himself at Riis' interest in money. He'd already suspected that Riis was a puppet who could be bought.

"It's not as straightforward as that, Supreme Commander.   Money for something on one's maximization path would be provided only if it is the fastest and easiest route to your maximization.

"We think we need money for every goal we want. Nature, however, is infinitely more creative. For example, one information coincidence might catapult you past hundreds of steps to your goal without the need for money. Accordingly, you'll want to be open to being orchestrated by the bioflow to achieving your goal through any channel rather than insisting it come through a specific channel such as money.

"The goal of the internal-external maximizing machinery is to keep you in savantflow, your maximum state. Period. You'll have to build your money goal in the direction that the bioflow is heading in order to benefit from it.

"I've already identified each living being as an information system," continued Connor. "Now I want you to think of creativity in information terms as well. *Creativity, creation, innovation, inventiveness, and creative breakthroughs are the result of combining existing information systems to create a new novel information system.*

"Think of the merging of a system of DNA information from each parent to create a new novel information system, a child. This recombining of information systems is how breakthroughs and epiphanies occur.

"This means that one will need easy access to the right information fuel to generate the breakthroughs necessary to solve Annutia's crises quickly. If you'll allow the bioflow to orchestrate your direction, you'll find yourself colliding with the exact information you need at the time you need it to re-combine for creative breakthroughs, flashes of genius, and Eureka events. This happens automatically with savantflow-bioflow integration.

"Over time, the magnitude, speed, quantity, quality, and impact of your breakthroughs will increase. Again, one breakthrough could eliminate hundreds of steps to achieve needed solutions faster. One breakthrough can change the world. One breakthrough can save a world in crisis. This means that even the ordinary can achieve the extraordinary.

"Obviously, the access to information fuel is key to the kind of serial breakthroughs we need to address Annutia's crises. Let me explain how I discovered how to increase the fuel to increase the breakthroughs.

"Mysteriously, savants usually display genius in one of five general fields — music, art, calendar recall or computation, mathematics, or mechanical/visual-spatial skills. A *music savant* may be able to perform an entire piece of music flawlessly after hearing it only once. Or, they may be able to play an instrument perfectly with no instruction or practice. Or, they may be able to demonstrate having an extensive repertoire of songs or pieces many of which they may never have heard before.

"*Calendar savants* can quickly identify the day of the week, the weather, and events for any calendar date past or present. *Mathematical savants* may be able to do rapid, complex calculations and equations in their heads in seconds. They can suddenly know the right mathematical answer even though most have brains incapable of even simple arithmetic.

"It gradually became obvious to me that most savants share a common skill – access to massive amounts of field-specific information which include procedural instructions. Savant superskills are information-based. Information and savantism are intimately linked. In some cases, the information base is itself the savant superskill as in *mnemonist savants*. Mnemonists have the ability to provide long lists of data such as names, numbers, entries in books, and so on."

"Do you mean a savant like Dustin Hoffman played in the movie *Rain Man*?" asked Axl.

"Precisely, Minister Plenipotentiary." Connor was delighted to discover another movie lover and another commonality with Axl. "Though fictional, he's the most famous savant. He's a composite of a few true savants.

"Through Raymond Babbitt, many of us were introduced to savants and learned what the human mind is capable of doing. You could see how Raymond was dysfunctional for so many things, but for capabilities based on access to a large database of information, he was a genius."

"Well, he must have been smart in some way to do the mathematical calculations he did," conjectured Rikard Riis.

"Or did he simply access calculations already in existence in a database of all potential calculations, Supreme Commander?" speculated Connor. His brain was too damaged to do the calculations or to retain the massive amounts of information which he demonstrated.

"I puzzled over why so many savants had precisely the same capabilities despite the variations in the damage to their left brains. Why did they access the same five or so databases of information? And why did those who acquired savantism later in life due to left-brain injury, suddenly know the same information about one of the savant field as other savants when they didn't know it before their injury?

"And why did so many savants access this information even though neuroscientists were able to prove that, like Raymond Babbitt, their brains should not be able to retain such information even if they could acquire it? This was all too coincidental to be simply an individual capability. Something larger and more universal was going on.

"It suddenly occurred to me that every savant was downloading a single book or system of information from an external library specific to the field of their genius or talent. Suddenly, everything fit. Savants in each of the five fields of genius were downloading precisely the same book. If the book didn't exist how could they all have access to that same book? The information had to be externally sourced. This is why I now call my overdrive achievement methodology *savanting*.

"In savantflow, we automatically connect to the information database relevant to the activity which has generated the flow state. Therefore, we have many more breakthroughs when we're in savantflow. We have access to more information fuel relevant to our task at hand which can be re-combined to generate breakthroughs."

Azurite Chief of State Einar Nyhus looked up from researching on his tablet. "Savant genius could indeed be externally sourced. There is nothing in the Annutia or Earth databases which demonstrates that scientists have discovered mechanisms internal to savant brains which proves how their genius occurs.

"In fact, the study of savant brains has demonstrated the opposite – that savants should not be able to do the amazing things that they do. Commander Kane's explanation may indeed be the more plausible one."

"Thank you, Minister Nyhus. Creativity from non-creatives becomes possible with this new modus operandi," continued Kane. "As with savants, the quantity and quality of the breakthroughs is not limited by one's intelligence, experience, or creativity.

"Rather it has to do with the access to information that results from integrating into the bioflow of nature's larger maximizing process. This automatically occurs in savantflow which is built into everyone. It is everyone's maximum state. Therefore, we could recruit an army of both creatives and non-creatives alike to help solve the Annutia crises.

"In addition, integration into the bioflow enables one's creativity to be guided in the direction of humanity's evolutionary flow. This means that the breakthroughs one will have will be important to the evolving human race. This integration is why a Bill Gates, Steve Jobs, or Jeff Bezos could invent at the front end of the evolution of civilization thus ensuring their products and services would be popular. They lived in savantflow.

"Therefore, connecting to the bioflow is how we'll ensure that we'll have the specific breakthroughs necessary to save Annutia. The bioflow is already trying to correct the damaged living systems of the planet. If we tap into that, our efforts will be synergistic with nature's efforts.

"To enter flow or savantflow, one must be stretched beyond one's previous capabilities. Consequently, growth is built in. The more time you spend in savantflow, the faster your functionality and strengths will increase. Therefore, over time, your system's maximum will increase.

"Because flow is an altered state of consciousness, one's consciousness will also develop over time. Specifically, serial savantflow sessions will cause your consciousness or breadth of perspective to expand.

"What does this mean for you? "If you're sitting in a rowboat on a river, your view of the events in your life might be like seeing boxes float past you. However, if you're in a hot air balloon above the river, you might see a pattern in those boxes or that they're connected into a system. From a plane you might be able to see that that system of boxes was connected to four other systems upon which you might capitalize to meet your goals.

"Eventually continuous expansion will lead each individual to experience unity consciousness. This means you can see and capitalize on the interconnectedness of all things for each territory upon which you choose to focus.

The solutions you can contribute to the world from this state will increase exponentially. With unity consciousness and immersion into the bioflow, you'll have more information upon which to make decisions. You'll also have more information to combine into new information systems.

"In addition, expanded consciousness will also trigger a cascading increase in your baseline functionality. Especially your meta-competencies. Cognitive skills, for example, will improve. There'll be upgrades in abstract thinking, conceptual thinking, big-picture thinking, systems thinking, strategic thinking, mental agility, adaptivity, pattern recognition, trend perception, environmental scanning, problem re-framing, and ambiguity resolution.

"Now imagine this kind of accelerated growth across Annutia's entire pool of human resources. You'll have raised the bar on the potential, the quality of life, and the operation of your entire civilization. You'll have made everyone's life more meaningful and contributory. You'll have linked everyone to the bioflow guidance system, so they're being orchestrated to the advantage of humanity."

"At this point, a global transformation will occur," continued Connor. He felt his frequency rising and those in the room coming with him as he continued to reveal compelling logic while bringing them to an emotional home innate in everyone.

"What will have emerged is a singular creative, inventive force directed by nature's evolutionary flow. The need for government control and direction will dissipate into distributed power and leadership. With every human being maximized in savantflow and moving with the bioflow, you'll have created unified direction and unified consciousness. You'll have a civilization based upon a single shared consciousness and purpose.

"Flow is an egoless state in which all that exists is the activity at hand. It is characterized by only positive emotions. Identity and separation cease to exist. Discrimination and conflict can therefore no longer exist. War will disappear. The fractionalization and segmentation of your society will fall away in this nature-run, talent-maximized world.

"Your society will have achieved spontaneous unification. All will become one. A single synergistic and synchronized oneness will emerge for the advance of humanity. *Universal peace and love would now be achievable as a byproduct of individual self-actualization and fulfillment.*"

At this point, Connor was unable to speak further. His eyes were moist with tears. He embraced them all in his vibration. Tears had welled up in each person's eyes in sympathetic vibration as they were bathed in the emotions of awe and love and feelings yet to be named.

Spontaneous knowledge had emerged for Connor from his savantflow that caused overwhelming emotion. He suddenly left the Council Chamber. No one could move.

They were each mesmerized by the possibilities and the emotions and frequencies that they were experiencing. They were unified into a single consciousness. All fractionalization had disappeared from themselves, from the room, and from the planet. Oneness. Omneity. It was indescribable.

Axl was the first to shatter the silence. "Annalise!"

"On it, Minister," she called from the darkness at the back of the auditorium as she dashed after Connor.

6

THE REUNION

Connor paced impatiently at the elevator. When Annalise caught up to him, she asked, "What has upset you, Commander?" He didn't respond. He didn't look up. He pressed the elevator button again in his agitation.

Since her direct approach had failed, Connor watched her slip into her usual indirect approach that he'd first witnessed on the trip from the wormhole to his residence. Annalise attempted to change his mood by distracting him with meaningful discourse on subjects that were dear to his heart.

Transformation to one's greatest work, for example. He had to admit, she had a gift for it. Unfortunately, she had violated his trust and he couldn't bring himself to forgive her yet.

"What you did at Council was incredible," Annalise proclaimed breathless from having run after him. He wasn't listening. His thoughts were elsewhere as he quickly got onto the elevator. She followed him in and took hold of him by the shoulders. She turned him to her to ensure he would focus on what she was saying.

"Commander, that was life-changing. No one in the room will ever be the same again." Connor pretended he wasn't listening, but she was undeterred.

"Your logic was compelling for sure. But something else happened to me because something was shifting in you as you got deeper into your savantflow. It was as if I was reset to my true self. My core frequency. It was just like those who've had near-death experiences. They come back knowing who they are and what they are meant to do with their lives. They then strip down their lives to that singular focus.

"Then towards the end I could feel your frequency increasing and I was being lifted with you. Then, all of a sudden, my vision expanded. Not gradually. Instantly. Like a switch had turned on unity consciousness. I became one with everything. It was as if I was no longer confined by my skin. And it was from that expanded perspective that I glimpsed my true purpose. I knew the meaning and goal of my life and indeed all life. I felt my immersion in the bioflow."

Annalise paused searching for words as if what she had said was inadequate. "Not as me, but as if I and the bioflow were one. Actually, it was more like I, Annalise, had disappeared into the pure creative expression of what was the essence of me. Only creativity or creative acts existed. The whole world became a single creative pulse or advance or evolution or act," she said as she struggled to describe the indescribable. "Immersion in the bioflow is shared creation," she suddenly exclaimed.

She was so bang on that Connor could not resist. He forgot his mood. "Perfect, Annalise. Thank you for that great term. I think 'shared creation' works far better for the masses than physicist David Bohm's 'holomovement.' In his 1980s book, 'Wholeness and the Implicate Order', he was trying to infuse the holistic principle of 'undivided wholeness' with the idea that everything is in a state of process or becoming. 'Shared creation' gives actionable purpose to Bohm's term of 'universal flux.'

"This immersion into shared creation is really what savanting is about, isn't it, Commander?"

"You have grasped the essence, Annalise." Connor was truly impressed with her depth of comprehension. It was exceedingly rare.

"It's a methodology for how to get back into the universe's creative process from cultures which have separated us from it," she continued.

"Yes. On the practical front, it's how to increase one's creative impact, contribution, and legacy by harnessing the creative flow of the universe."

"This is what I'm meant to do, Commander. What you do. This is why the bioflow has brought me here. It was so fortuitous that the Minister Plenipotentiary assigned me to work on your mission. It's a tribute to his talent for seeing what people are meant to do before they even know what that is."

Given Connor's experience with Axl persuading him to take on this mission, he had to agree. "It's as if Dahl is already integrated into the bioflow and doing its bidding."

Connor realized he had succumbed to Annalise's efforts to distract him and calm him down. "Annalise, Lenore is in a suite two floors down from mine and five suites over. I must go to her."

"How do you know?" queried Annalise as they negotiated the busy concourse on the way to the elevator for the residential tower.

"Spontaneous knowledge in savantflow," replied Connor without his usual translation for those not fluent in savanting. Finally, he knew the reason for the puzzled look on Annalise's face when Axl asked her to arrange a phone call with Lenore. Annalise had known Lenore was here but didn't tell him. He considered this a major betrayal even though another part of him knew full well that she had orders not to tell him.

"Remote viewing," blurted Connor to give her more specifics. "I could see what Lenore was seeing.

As I reached savantflow during my speech, I suddenly had a flash of her view from the window of her suite and noticed it was similar to mine but slightly lower and further along."

"This was the 'remote view' code she had referenced in our call. Lenore was trying to remind me of our ability since childhood for remote viewing through each other's eyes no matter what the distance between us. I'd forgotten because we've so rarely been apart for decades. As soon as I realized Lenore was here, I had to go to her."

Annalise followed Connor into the residence elevator. He repeatedly pressed the floor for Lenore in his impatience. Nothing was said. When he came off the elevator, he immediately saw Niels protecting a door five suites closer to the elevator than his own. Connor went to this door.

"Lenore. Lenore. It's Connor. Can you hear me?

"Connor. You found me. You figured out my clue."

"Yes, my love. Are you okay? "

"I'm fine. I can't believe you're here."

"Can you open the door, Lenore?"

"No. I'm locked in from the outside."

As Connor braced himself to crash in the door, Niels looked at Annalise for instructions.

She shrugged. "Let him in, Niels." Niels keyed the pass code and opened the door. Connor brushed past him. Lenore was there. His beautiful Lenore. He scooped her into his arms. They clung to each other in silence, tears streaming down.

After several moments passed, Connor released Lenore and broke the silence.

"Lenore, this is Annalise.

Annalise. It's my pleasure," said Lenore warmly as she shook her hand.

"Annalise is helping us with our new mission."

"We have a mission?" questioned Lenore with her teasing eyes dancing on his.

"Yes, another mission-critical project of planetary significance," sighed Connor facetiously.

"Connor, my love, I don't think you have this retirement thing quite figured out yet," Lenore quipped.

Connor was pleased that Lenore was still her usual fearless self and was unharmed.

"Annalise. Lenore is moving to my suite. Should we bring her things now or is there someone to do that?"

Despite his politeness, Connor knew he was not fully masking his icy reaction to Lenore being kidnapped first, imprisoned second, brought to a planet where they might die, third and now finally separated on top of all that so that she experienced more pain.

They both were diplomatic so there was not going to be an open argument between he and Annalise. However, he was fairly certain she sensed he wasn't pleased. He could also see that she didn't feel good about a situation in which she too was a victim. The lives of both he and his wife were now in danger on a dying planet.

"Leave it with me, Commander." While Lenore was out of earshot collecting some of her things from the bedroom, Annalise spoke to Connor in a lowered voice.

"I accept that the mission partnership I want with you, Commander, might now be in jeopardy. This breach of trust has been beyond my control. It may be a challenge for me to repair that trust, but I intend to do everything in my power to try. As I advised when we met, Commander, there will be information which I won't be authorized to share with you. Your wife was unfortunately part of that.

"However, Commander, it is more complicated than you're assuming. Lenore's abduction was not Minister Dahl's doing. Rather, it was the action of some darker forces on the Council who wanted leverage – leverage for what we don't know. This is why Jon, Brik, Niels, and I are doing what we can to protect you and Lenore. We can't have someone compromise or control you by using Lenore. I'll keep you apprised."

Connor nodded a knowing thanks. He felt he and Annalise were now good. Lenore returned from the other room with a large bag in her hand. All three left the suite. Connor and Lenore moved toward the elevator arm in arm and locked in their usual banter. Annalise issued instructions to Niels and then she hurried to catch up.

Brik was at Connor's door as they stepped off the elevator. Jon was closer to the elevator talking frantically on a communication device trying to locate Connor. He'd lost him at the Council meeting. Jon saw the trio coming.

"I have Phoenix," said Jon into the communicator. "He's back at his suite."

"Jon. Brik. This is my wife, Lenore. She'll be staying with me. It's important that you protect her as well."

"Yes, Commander," assured Brik. "It's a pleasure to meet you, Mrs. Kane. Welcome."

"Thank you, Brik," said Lenore warmly.

"Come, my love. Let's get caught up," said Connor taking her hand and sweeping her into his suite to the open kitchen. Connor took one of the tall leather stools at the counter while Lenore examined the cupboards, counters, and fridge for food.

They bantered back and forth quickly and familiarly as if nothing so drastic and traumatic had happened. Lenore brought out food trays from the fridge. They grazed.

"This is definitely not your cooking, Connor."

"I'm a good cook," Connor protested.

"How would I know? Name one thing I've eaten in the last decade that you cooked."

"Well you're a much more talented cook than I."

"You're just keeping me around for my cooking. I'm just your slave," she teased.

"My food is being prepared by a chef. See that gadget there on the counter. The next day's menus are listed there and you check off what you want."

"Very nice. I've had to cook for myself in my suite."

Lenore poured boiling water from a heated carafe into two mugs with tea bags and set one down in front of Connor along with a bowl of sweeteners. There was a knock on the door. It opened. It was Annalise and Niels bringing a large box of Lenore's things. Niels set it on a nearby chair.

"We'll leave you two alone to catch up," announced Annalise. "Commander, the Council has a number of questions. I'll pick you up at 8 am tomorrow to return to Council."

"Thanks, Annalise." The door closed.

"You have TVs, stereos, computer equipment, gym equipment, ... " Lenore exclaimed with delight as she explored the suite. She turned on the TV and increased the volume. She walked over to stand next to Connor still sitting on his high stool at the counter.

Lenore whispered in his ear, "I saw how the engineer ran the wormhole for the two vehicles that followed mine. I think I could get us home."

"Aren't you amazing. Are you sure?" Connor whispered.

"I asked the engineer all sorts of questions. He liked talking about his work." Lenore had always had a gift for getting people to talk about themselves.

"Can two people ride in one bubble without crashing into each other?" Connor wondered out loud.

"It was very calm in the center." commented Lenore.

"How'd you figure that out?" "It took me half the flight of smashing off the walls before I discovered the center. I still have the bruises."

"Some of us are just smarter than others," she winked.

"Who do you think was in the third bubble?"

"I didn't see who it was."

"Who would you have picked for a repeat of the save-the-Earth project," asked Connor.

"Daniel!" both said at the same time with smiles.

"But he's so young," worried mother-hen Lenore. Thirty-two?"

"Yes, but he operates from unity consciousness. He can see the patterns for the best direction for the teams to harness the bioflow. He knows how to combine the available information pieces for breakthroughs. I hope it's him."

"What if it's Royce Duncombe?" queried Lenore with distaste.

"He must be almost 55. But the world does love British aristocracy."

"Well, from the outside he might have looked like the person to replace you. He has the degrees, the connections, the breeding . . . ."

"He takes credit for the work of others. He doesn't actually do anything. He has no innate talent for the work. I suspect our abductors might have figured that out."

"I didn't see Royce at the reunion so he could have been taken already. Did you see him?"

"You're right. I didn't. But I wouldn't have expected him to pay tribute."

"But he would have schmoozed for your job, Connor."

"True. True. He wouldn't have missed that opportunity."

"Have you given your intro speech yet?"

"Yes, an hour or so ago."

"Did you do your raising-the-frequency thing?"

"You know I can't control that."

"I think that was true once. But now I think you put it on whenever you want to," she said, again with the teasing.

"Possibly, that might be true." He knew it was useless to lie to Lenore.

"So, let me tell you our mission if we don't want to die within the next year."

"Yes, please. Tell me more," she demanded enthusiastically.

Connor loved how Lenore embraced their plight fearlessly whenever they were together. They made a good team. She was his courage and he hers. They could conquer anything together. Until now, he wondered?

7

THE COUNCIL AFTERMATH

Annalise arrived at 8:00 a.m. as promised. Connor was ready. But so was Lenore.

"Do you think it's a good idea to have Lenore come, Commander?"

"I'm concerned about leaving her here alone, Annalise. After this scare, I don't relish having her out of my sight."

"I could get Niels."

"My preference is always to be open, honest, and transparent. In addition, I think Lenore's presence might help to uncover and perhaps undo any subterfuge associated with her being here."

"Right, Commander. That could be a good strategy. An intriguing unveiling. I'll watch for reactions from the Ministers. One other thing of which I must forewarn you is the lack of respect for the abilities of women. We're perhaps a half century behind Earth."

"Lenore, can you be quiet for the duration of the Council meeting and let the important men talk?" baited Connor with a glint in his eye.

"I promise to be good, Master," she flirted with a mischievous grin.

"You jest," he exclaimed good naturedly to Lenore. She jests," he feigned offence to Annalise with a shrug. Annalise laughed, obviously enjoying being part of their camaraderie.

"Okay, ladies. Let's get this inquisition over with," he said as he ushered them out of the suite.

"Good morning, Jon. Good morning, Brik."

"Good morning, Commander, Mrs. Kane" as Jon and Brik fell dutifully in behind them.

♦♦♦

As they entered the Council Chamber, everyone was busy finding their coffee, their breakfast, and greeting each other. The trio moved over to the refreshment bar and helped themselves. It didn't take Axl long to come over with a "Good Morning, Commander Kane."

"Good Morning, Minister Dahl. May I introduce my wife, Lenore?"

Axl reached out and shook Lenore's hand. "A pleasure, Lenore."

"How do you do, Minister," Lenore responded warmly, her eyes darting quickly between Axl and her husband. Connor saw that Lenore was visibly surprised by Axl's similarity to his own fair, angular, and athletic features. They were the same height. Axl could be Connor's father or at least a relative.

The Minister's face revealed nothing amiss. The man was unflappable thought Connor with admiration. He must have been the person whom Annalise had texted on the way over to forewarn him of Lenore's attendance.

"Annalise. Will you and Lenore take your seats, please? It's time to get started." Commander, unfortunately you're once more in the hot seat at the top of the table.

"Thank you, Minister," responded Connor as he moved to his chair.

Connor noticed that Annalise had taken Lenore to the audience seats outside of the bright lights of the Council table but not to the darkness in the back. He smiled at Lenore. She smiled back.

"It's time, Ministers," called Supreme Commander Rikard Riis. "Please take your seats." Riis sat down at the other head of the table. Axl took a seat to the left of Connor at the side of the head of table at the other end.

Supreme Commander Riis opened the meeting. "Are there questions or comments about yesterday's speech with respect to the pursuit of the inventiveness maximization project to resolve our current crises?"

"The Defense Coalition would like to register its opposition, Supreme Commander," said Defense Minister Karsten Kolbeck.

Grand Admiral Falk demonstrated agreement by saying, "We trust in Annutia's military strength. We feel we should gather an attack force to penetrate the wormholes going to other locations than Earth. We want to find and kill or disable whatever species is xenoforming our planet."

Grand General Haugstad, the head of the non-naval armed forces, refrained from comment. His silence spoke volumes about his disagreement.

The KahlDahr Chief of State, Lennart Lorenson, spoke up next. "Supreme Commander, if I may. This military strategy will alert our enemies. If they're more advanced than us, they'll not wait for the xenoforming to complete. They'll simply eradicate or enslave us and take the planet. We have no history of proactive attacks. Only defense. We'll be playing to our weaknesses to attack."

Axl nodded. "This is the reason I've brought Commander-in-Chief Kane here. If he can augment ingenuity among the Annutian tribes fast enough, we can covertly stop or transmute the xenoforming. We can prevent loss of life. We'll have time to research our enemy and develop strategies and weapons to defend ourselves and Annutia against them." The exchanges began to heat up.

Kolbeck argued in a louder voice than necessary, "Minister Dahl perpetually undervalues the military and the capabilities of our defense industry companies. Instead he is touting an unknown strategy that will take months to succeed."

Axl calmly defended his position. "My study of the Earth transformation at the hands of Commander Kane, shows an 800 per cent increase within the first three months of breakthrough inventions and inventiveness specific to averting their crises. There is no reason to think that this level and speed of performance could not be achieved on Annutia. Perhaps it is you, Minister Kolbeck, who is underestimating the Annutian people."

Grand General Haugstad finally joined into the fray with a voice of reason for his Military and Defense colleagues. "I would like to propose exploratory wormhole investigations to discover our enemy and evaluate the magnitude and character of their defenses. Rather than committing to start a war today, I think we should initiate a plan to discover who they are, how to beat them, and to determine our chances for winning a war."

"An excellent idea, Grand General," praised Axl.

Taking his cue from Axl's opinion, the new Supreme Commander Riis asked for a show of hands from all in favor of exploratory missions to find out who is xenoforming our planet, whether we can defeat them, and how.

As he motioned to each member around the table, all 12 agreed. Riis was obviously relieved that the warmongers had been appeased so he didn't need to take sides.

Luminary Ozias initiated the next topic. "I'm worried about religious interference. We would be handing over the education and growth of our people to an alien."

Connor was immediately mistrustful of the man. He seemed duplicitous. His air of reverence and concern as a religious leader seemed to be an act. To Connor, at least, the man seemed to be motivated by power and celebrity. This meant he would have to be extremely cautious with this man. Ozias might fly off the handle or provoke argument for dramatic effect rather than deal with the true issues at hand.

Connor had had the good fortune to meet some of Earth's greatest spiritual leaders. Ozias had none of their substance, grace, or wellspring of genuine benevolence, wisdom, and empathy. They had all experienced exalted states. They had a certain aura and ambience as a result. This depth and expansiveness were missing in Ozias.

Connor felt there were ulterior motives to Ozias' current opposition. What could he be trying to achieve? How could Connor avoid falling into the trap he sensed Ozias was trying to set? Connor took a guess and formulated a strategy for protecting himself and his work.

He chose his words very carefully so as not to incite the drama he sensed Ozias was seeking. He strategized that if he never separated from Ozias' position – if he never became the person in opposition to Ozias' position – that perhaps the conflict – or, was it more, the power trip – that the religious leader seemed to be seeking could be averted.

Connor began to humbly but logically address the religious leader. "Luminary Ozias, I'm going to assume that my credentials have already been vetted for this position before I was invited." Connor decided not to use the inflammatory term of 'abducted.'

"May I assure you, your Grace, that I'm 100% confident that I can entirely circumvent your realm of operation. Minister Dahl has been very clear about my mission. It is to engender Annutian talent and ingenuity to solve the crises threatening your world. This entails communicating a set of skills and a modus operandi for taking action.

"I am offering an achievement discipline not reliant on anything developed by religious or spiritual disciplines. It's simply a different way to operate that yields peak performance, spontaneous knowledge, creative inspirations, flashes of genius, and breakthroughs. It's neither my place nor my interest nor my talent nor has it been my historical background to imprint religious or spiritual beliefs. I'm here simply to educate on a new way to operate that will incite the breakthroughs needed to save your world."

Ozias seemed genuinely disappointed that Connor had done such a good job at disarming the drama and conflict he craved. However, he seemed unprepared to give up on his cause, whatever that might be.

"Religions have been in the people development business for a long time, Commander Kane. It's hard to imagine that you could have developed something entirely new," prodded Ozias, continuing to try to discredit Connor, for what goal, Connor still could not grasp.

"I know of no area of overlap or conflict, Luminary Ozias," Connor responded in keeping with his strategy not to separate.

Still not satisfied, Ozias continued. "For example, we have a very specific path to unity consciousness and knowing God, Commander Kane. From your speech, you appear to be offering an alternative route. This would be interference with our teachings, would it not?"

The attack continues sighed Connor. "If you position electrodes correctly in a person's brain, they will spontaneously experience unity consciousness. It's physiologically built into human beings. It doesn't require spiritual disciplines or practices or states of religious evolution to get there.

"My method is more natural and long-lasting because it emerges as a byproduct of the altered consciousness of savantflows as one continues to deepen with them over time. Eventually unity consciousness will become one's normal state of being because that is what is innate in everyone.

"Unity consciousness is simply a broadened perspective. One can achieve superior performance in unity consciousness because one can see the interconnectedness of all things. One has access to more information to be recombined to create novelty and invention. Therefore, it is an ideal goal for an achievement technology such as ours.

"Strictly from a biological perspective, the highest level of consciousness is an egoless, identityless, nonseparation state of pure creative expression. If you're going to merge into oneness with everything, there can be no separation. There could be no sense of self whatsoever. God could not be a separate entity. One is simply fused with the creative act at hand. One is fully integrated into the creative pulse of the universe.

"Since unity consciousness is an egoless state of nonseparation, practices that require one to keep a sense of self or to know God as a separate entity will interfere with achieving that egoless state. If you have that conflict in your religion, that's for you to sort out, Luminary Ozias, as you decide on your goals for your people.

"Are you suggesting that our religious and spiritual practices are interfering? retorted Ozias indignantly.

"Not at all, your Eminence. I am simply explaining why I will neither be using your methods nor interfering with them. If both of our methods want people to achieve unity consciousness, then the unity consciousness byproduct of my modus operandi would support the goals of your religions without interfering in any way with its dogma. Would we not then be partners rather than adversaries?"

Luminary Ozias was too furious to answer. Connor had unintentionally made an enemy. Why wondered Connor? In a flash he knew the answer. Despite his intent to bond and allay fears, Connor had accidentally pulled the curtain aside on the religious leader's façade of spiritual enlightenment.

Connor suddenly realized, that Ozias must never have experienced the oneness of unity consciousness. He was preaching unity consciousness without ever having experienced it. Otherwise, he would not have made the mistake of trying to protect separateness and fragmentation.

Oops! thought Connor. The 1785 poem of Robert Burns ran through his mind. 'The best-laid plans of mice and men go oft awry.' Since Ozias knew that Connor routinely operated from unity consciousness, it was likely that Ozias would always resent him. He would have to accept that there may not be anything Connor could do to prevent his animosity going forward.

"If I make any missteps which interfere with your planet's religious practices, Luminary Ozias, I would be most appreciative of your counsel." No response. Connor glanced over at Lenore. Both she and Annalise seemed pleased with his responses to the inquisition. Axl was beaming with pride.

As Connor looked into the depths of the beautiful burled wood of the Council table, he realized, for a second time, that he was on board with helping these people. In convincing others, he'd inadvertently further sold himself on their mission. Connor felt again an unexpected sense of transformation.

The Council broke briefly for nature and refreshment.

8

THE DRUG CARTELS

All delegates returned to the Council table. Pieter Holst, the Minister-in-Charge of the Pharmaceuticals Coalition, spoke next. "The Pharmaceutical Coalition would also like to register its opposition. "Minister Plenipotentiary Dahl," Holst admonished, "you're forcing us to accept a strategy that you inflicted on us as a final gasp of your term of office as Supreme Commander.

"You're trying to subvert government process and due diligence. You're interfering with free market economics and corporate revenues and patents by offering a competing solution and by denigrating our smart drug campaign."

It occurred to Connor that this was a war begun a long time ago which had now escalated. Holst's accusations were acerbic but, as usual, the imperturbable Minister Dahl did not respond in kind.

"You may recall Minister Holst," he continued calmly, "that Commander Kane had a security detail of six federal agents and lived in a government compound patrolled by the military. In many ways, he was more protected than the American President.

"His retirement gala was the Commander's first public appearance unprotected in ten years. We responded immediately to that very first opportunity to collect him. Your attribution of motivations of personal interests to me at the end of my term are therefore unfounded."

"What about the Smart Drug program? We've seen considerable success. Why is the government not buying more drugs from us to help people to address the crises?

"May I, Supreme Commander?" asked Axl deferentially.

"By all means," responded Riis relieved to be out of the line of fire.

"It's my job to think of what is good for the entire Annutian population. Some improvement in cognitive performance has been demonstrated with your smart drugs, especially with Ultra. However, these improvements did not include upgrades to creativity. They haven't yielded any breakthroughs over the last year to solve our crises. A year is long enough for us to determine whether smart drugs will be of benefit. They are not the solution.

"In addition, some rather severe side effects have begun to appear which go far beyond the problems we foresaw of creating addicts and all the side effects that that syndrome entails. And thirdly, a lot of our budget is now constrained by the need to address the water, power, and food shortages precipitated by the speedy progression of the xenoforming.

"Commander Kane, I believe Annalise has brought you up-to-date on the smart drug campaign. Would you be so kind as to articulate the comparison with your approach? I'm afraid I would not do it justice."

"Of course, Minister Dahl. Biochemistry and neuroscience are not my areas of expertise, Minister Holst, so please accept my apologies in advance for the simplicity of my representations."

In truth, Connor wanted to ensure that everyone in the room understood his points in the briefest amount of time. Simplicity is key. At least five of the twelve Council members had looked like deer in headlights at the mere mention of smart drugs.

Anxious to make his pitch, Holst immediately tried to wrest the floor from Connor. "Why don't I describe the drugs and the campaign?"

Connor suspected that the Ministers had heard the pitch before and their eyes had likely glazed over. There is a reason why the Council members were uncomfortable talking about smart drugs. It was likely that Holst's methods of communication were the issue.

Probably too technical. Sometimes even the best communicators can get too close to a subject.

Movies, Connor had discovered, were an excellent shorthand that quickly conveyed a breadth of information. The screenwriters had already done most of his work. Accordingly, he had had Annalise help him to research relevant Earth movies that were also popular on Annutia.

Accordingly, Connor held his ground. "Minister Holst, if I do the summary myself, I will be able to demonstrate that I understand. This will lend credence to my comparison of your smart-drug approach to my revised-modus-operandi approach." Pieter Holst reluctantly nodded and Connor retained the floor.

"I will explain in greater detail in a minute but here are the bullet points of the key differences with my approach:

a) an enhancement to the engine for creativity, the right brain, and

b) an increase in the information fuel to feed that engine.

c) an increase in the quantity and depth of savantflows, a peak performance state arguably beyond the capacity of your smart drugs.

d) the benefits of unity consciousness and improved cognitive skills which emerge as savantflow states increase in frequency and depth. And finally,

e) the ability of savanting to strengthen and empower all of Annutia's human assets versus a limited distribution of smart drugs and the disadvantage that they kill or diminish human assets.

"There are three popular smart-drug movies on Earth which I discovered are also popular here: *Limitless* (2011), *The Bourne Legacy* (2012), and *Lucy* (2014). Let's start with *Limitless*.

"Your Ultra seeks the increased ability to intake, retain, and process information that struggling writer, Edward Morra, experiences when he ingests the cognition-enhancing drug called NZT-48. This was an experimental drug to increase his performance by enabling him to access one hundred percent of his brain abilities. As a result, a struggling writer becomes a financial wizard.

"The movie claims that we ordinarily only use 20% of our brains. The goal of cognitive enhancements and the fictional NZT-48 is to let us use all of it. The flaw in the logic here is that there is no guarantee that there are benefits from simply increasing the percentage of brain use.

"The real challenge is to identify the ideal parts of the brain to be activated for creative solutions to Annutia's crises which is what savanting does.

"The movie, *Lucy*, also tries to tie the progression of human and then superhuman functionality to the increase in the percentage of the brain utilized. There has been no such progression demonstrated by Ultra. That is because Ultra targets specific areas of the brain.

"This is where *The Bourne Legacy* explains more specifically how Ultra works. Jeremy Renner's character, Aaron Cross, loses his 'chems' in the opening scenes which sets his path to find the replacements necessary for his mission before he loses the potency of what is already in his system.

"Cross takes different color pills for different enhancements. Your smart drug, Minister Holst, targets specific enhancements in the same way. As in *The Bourne Legacy* movie, Ultra appears to also use viral material like a suitcase to load everything required for genetic change into a person at the precise target DNA site. This targeting is possible because of improvements in genetic and viral receptor mapping.

"However, based on Minister Dahl's description of results, it would seem that the right-brain sites associated with inventiveness and creativity have not yet been identified and thus not yet addressed by Ultra. I'm sure these sites will be discovered with time," Connor said encouragingly with neither judgement nor criticism.

Pieter Holst's jaw dropped. It appeared to Connor that he had surprised the head of the Pharmaceutical Coalition by precisely deducing the flaw of their smart drug campaign, despite all their efforts to keep it out of the official reports which Connor had been allowed to read.

"However, in the meantime," Connor continued, "as the length of use increases, the negative side effects identified in *Limitless* are starting to emerge with Ultra. In addition, severe mental rebound effects are now becoming the norm even if the drugs are stopped.

"Quick physical, emotional, and psychological decline is evident. The death toll of those on Ultra or having been on Ultra but stopped is also increasing. When a whole civilization is facing eradication, perhaps this is a risk to be tolerated." Connor shrugged as animation to his unspoken question.

"Minister Nyhus identified a fourth movie, the winner of best picture of 1988, *Rain Man*. This helps to identify the cognitive advantages of my approach over smart drugs. Raymond Babbitt is perhaps the world's most famous savant. He was formulated from the attributes of multiple savants.

"Through Raymond, many of us learned for the first time what the human mind is capable of doing. Lightening quick mathematical calculations. Encyclopedic recitations. Flawless musical recitals or artwork replications after only one exposure. As with so many savants, Babbitt also has calendar recall or calendar-calculating skills.

Savant skills are all the more amazing for emerging from individuals with cognitive limitations. Their left brains are damaged.

"They don't have the brain function necessary to access, retain, and execute the massive amounts of information upon which their genius is based. Therefore, we can assume that they are accessing the information and procedures externally.

"They can access a manual of procedural information and data in a specific field – music, mathematics, calendar, and such – from the library database underpinning or defining humanity.

"Normals do the same when in my savantflow – except the information fuel for the creativity engine is a manual extremely relevant to the task at hand which has produced their flow state. It's the right information at the right time to be recombined for breakthroughs that can catapult you to your goals of saving the planet.

"My approach targets creativity and serial breakthroughs that progress along related synergistic channels such as a field or frontier."

Connor glanced at Axl for audience feedback. He was beaming again. He was obviously pleased with his choice in *recruiting* Connor.

"I've also indicated that there is a built-in progression to deeper savantflows leading to unity consciousness and more advanced cognitive functioning such as meta-skill development. As a result, the baseline functionality of the individual will be continually increasing.

The individual's peak performance will be continually increasing. And this growth in functionality is sustainable. It won't disappear if access to a smart drug is lost.

"In addition, having an expanded consciousness will enable one to view the interconnectedness of all relevant systems. This means it will be easier to see how to re-combine existing information systems to create a new breakthrough system. One's breakthroughs, epiphanies, and flashes of genius will thus increase.

"I hope I have provided an understanding of why my process may provide greater solutions to the crises than your smart drug campaign, Minister Holst. But the important thing is that neither program will interfere with the other or with religion, Luminary Ozias," Connor said as he turned towards the religious leader. "They can all three co-exist without conflict or interference."

Everyone in the Council Chamber was excited by the potential for solutions offered by Commander Connor Kane. This was the first good news they'd had for some time with respect to the survival of the planet. They stood and moved toward Connor with comments of congratulations, commendations, and gratitude, introductory handshakes, and well-intended pats on his person.

Out of the corner of his eye, Connor caught a glimpse of Pieter Holst sitting alone in his seat glaring at Minister Dahl. If looks could kill thought Connor. He suspected that by association, he, too, was getting virtual daggers. Connor had used his most deft shrewdness in neither competing with the smart drug campaign nor precluding it. He and Dahl had unfortunately won against Holst today rather than bringing him onboard with Connor's mission. Holst's failure was likely to bring unavoidable retaliation. No amount of graciousness on their part was going to change that.

9
THE RECRUITING

Precisely at 9:00 am, as promised, Annalise knocked on their suite door.

"Come in," called Lenore from laying out breakfast on the island counter in the open-concept kitchen.

"Good morning, Annalise. So, what did the Council decide?"

"Let's wait for Connor," said Annalise.

Lenore called to Connor in the bedroom.

"What did she say?" Connor called back.

"Nothing. I'm *persona non-grata*," said Lenore winking at Annalise. "We need the great Commander Kane before we can get any information."

"Coming," called Connor as he entered the living room while tucking in his shirt.

"Good morning, Commander Kane. The Council was very pleased with the potential of the talent mobilization and maximization program that you outlined yesterday for our survival. Congratulations. They approved your campaign. You've been allocated a budget of $10 million to start," said Annalise as she laid a heavy document on the counter."

"That would be for me," said Lenore picking up the document. She pointed to Connor. "Talent." She pointed to herself. "Management."

"According to the procedures outlined in Appendix 1 of your dossier," continued Annalise with a professional demeanor, "your next step is the recruitment of your creative and execution teams. Accordingly, I've brought supplies." She opened the suite door and Brik came in with extra laptops, tablets, cell phones, printer paper, folders, and other office supplies.

"I'll help you get access to our human resources database so you may get started with the selection of your people."

"I've already picked out a few people I saw in the Government Complex," said Connor. "Can I take Jon or Brik and go around to interview them?"

"I never saw you talk to anyone," said a puzzled Annalise.

"I'm very observant," confessed Connor. "Occupational hazard. I'm always looking for people for my campaigns."

"Trust him," chimed in Lenore. "Connor is uncanny when it comes to identifying those who will excel at savantflows within the bioflow. It defies logic, Annalise. Just accept."

"Very well, Commander. I'll help Lenore to access our database while Niels and Jon escort you." She immediately sent a text.

Connor grabbed grapes and cheese from Lenore's breakfast buffet to eat on the way. He also snagged a few confidentiality agreements from the stack he saw Brik bring in.

"Oh, Annalise," Connor called as he left the suite. "If Daniel Lowe was the third person kidnapped from Earth, we could use him now. In the adjoining suite would be perfect . . . ."

Connor and his entourage arrived at the front desk of the adjoining Planetary Government Complex. "I'm looking for someone who works in the building named Kellin. Do you know him?" asked Connor.

"Do you mean the janitor, sir?" asked the Concierge.

"Is he a tall robust man, stooped, black hair, . . . ?"

"With a protruding brow?"

Connor nodded.

"Yes," responded the Concierge looking at his screen. "He's in the machine room on the roof fixing the air conditioning system."

"That is pretty advanced work for a janitor," commented Connor.

"Well, when the engineers can't fix something, Kellin works on it," responded the Concierge without realizing he had confirmed Connor's insight.

"It sounds like Kellin should be more than a janitor," observed Connor.

"Well, he is KahlDahr," said the Concierge. "They have limited smarts. They're best suited to working with their hands."

"All evidence to the contrary," said Connor. He'd always had difficulty hiding his contempt for prejudice. He loved talent in any form it presented.

"What do you mean, sir?" asked the Concierge.

"Could you tell Kellin we're on our way up, please," as he headed towards the elevator with Jon and Niels.

On the elevator ride to his first meeting with Axl, Connor had overheard Kellin explaining to the engineers how he'd *MacGyvered* the building's plumbing system to overcome the low-pressure problem. He was concerned that they might undo his fix. The engineers were obviously impressed with his ingenuity.

As the trio entered the machine room, Connor spotted Kellin working on a large machine.

"Kellin. My name is Connor Kane." Kellin continued working without looking up.

"I wanted to find out more about you."

"Are you Human Resources?" asked Kellin gruffly. Again, not looking up from his work.

"In a way. How'd you come by your expertise for fixing systems?"

"I've always been fascinated by how machinery works. As a child, there was an old car pushed onto our lawn at home when it had died a decade before. I liked to tinker with it. To take it apart and put it back together so I would know how it works.

"Eventually, I figured out what was wrong, found all the parts at a nearby junkyard and was the first of my friends at age 12 to own a car. No one taught me. I just kind of knew. People used to tease me that I was a new kind of child prodigy. Mechanical.

"My neighbor was an engineer who worked at a nearby factory fixing all sorts of big machinery. I would always pester him to take me to work with him so I could watch him fix these massive systems. I would ask a million questions. Whenever I saw him, we'd always talk about how various systems worked or how to fix various problems. Eventually, he let me help him repair machines at his work. It became my after-school job.

"I began to figure out what was wrong before the engineers did and I came up with unique solutions for getting machines up and working again quickly even when parts were missing. I was an expert at what they call *jury rigging*. Gradually, I'd made a name for myself. They began calling for me directly without my neighbor. Other factories too. I loved it.

"Eventually, I craved the big systems that run this massive complex of Planetary Government buildings. These are the largest on the planet. Unfortunately, they'd only bring me on as a janitor. The KahlDahr are the lowest caste. It's assumed that we're only suited to menial work."

"Surely, they have come to see your talent," said Connor with surprise.

"The engineers know, for sure. But I suspect they pretty much take credit for my repairs. I don't really have occasion to talk with the *suits*."

"Why do you stay?" asked Connor.

"Once I have completed my janitorial duties, I secretly explore and fix these massive machines that I love. That challenges me to continuously surpass myself. I enjoy it when the engineers with their impressive degrees go home in frustration having failed to make the necessary repairs. Then, I can work into the night and fix what they could not. I just have a rapport with these systems. Each has a personality. Each is a friend."

Connor liked this strikingly handsome late thirty-something man. He was full of the benevolent energy, wonderment, curiosity, talent, and creativity that Connor was seeking.

The expansiveness of his thinking to crave such massive systems suggested Kellin had frequently experienced serial savantflows – probably since that first car. He represented the waste of talent based on outdated classifications, segregations, and discriminations.

"Kellin, I have a proposition for you that will most certainly change your life. To tell you about it, I need to ask you to sign this confidentiality agreement."

Kellin turned from his work to look Connor full in the eye for several seconds to get a measure of the man. "For whatever reason, I trust you, Connor Kane," he said signing the paper.

"Could you step out, please, Jon and Niels?"

♦ ♦ ♦

A half-hour later, the two men were shaking hands. The air conditioner was fixed. Connor had not only recruited Kellin Bergh but his nineteen-year-old son, Rolland, as well who had apparently inherited his father's genius and passion. The trio moved next to the programming floor. There was a girl there that Connor liked. He recruited five more people before returning to the suite for lunch.

"Hello everyone. I'm back," called Connor.

Lenore came out of the office. "Would you believe we've identified almost 150 candidates? Annalise has a clerical team setting up interviews as we speak."

"I locked down seven this morning, said Connor. And they're good. 150 to interview? How is that even possible, Lenore?"

"Annalise was a big help. Do you know she has more degrees than we do to do this work? I also had some other help." All of a sudden, a tall, dark and handsome young man walked out into the living room.

"Daniel!" cried Connor. "You're here." The two hugged. "I'm both happy and unhappy that you're here. I guess you know already that it's life or death this time around. I half-wish they picked Royce Duncombe in case we fail."

"With Royce you would have failed." All three laughed. "With me, you won't. We're the A-Team," declared Daniel jovially with pride.

10

THE ATTACK

The entourage was getting larger. Brik, Jon and Annalise were now protecting Lenore, Connor and Daniel after a good day of conducting Breakthru School. After leaving the elevator in the Planetary Government building, they began walking across the concourse to the elevator for the residential tower.

Jon was in front checking the way forward. Brik brought up the rear. Lenore had her arm linked through Connor's as they chatted about the events of the day. Behind them, Daniel was flirting with Annalise as usual. Brik brought up the rear.

No one noticed when Brik disappeared. Consequently, no one was prepared for the sudden attack on Jon, knocking him out with a single bludgeoning as he passed the next corridor. Lenore screamed as she saw what was happening. Suddenly the remaining entourage was locked between two gunmen.

"Please come with us," one of the gunmen said politely but firmly. He motioned to turn right at the next adjoining corridor. Connor turned to look at Annalise. She nodded to him in the forward direction. Initially he took that to mean that they should comply. Then suddenly the calm graceful Annalise was alive with Asian martial arts of some sort wiping out the back gunmen with kicks and hits from every angle in rapid succession.

This was such unexpected fierce fury coming from Annalise, the elegant diplomat. Like a tigress protecting her young. It surprised Connor how personal this was for her. This was not someone doing her job. This was someone who genuinely cared for them.

Annalise had been facing the forward gunman. Without even turning around she began a corkscrew spin whereby, with one kick of her right leg, she sent the gun flying 20 feet away. Now almost facing the unarmed gunman in her corkscrew spin, her left arm came forward to accomplish a knuckle chop to the windpipe. He doubled over with a look of extreme surprise.

Attack. Attack. Attack. Left hand. Left leg. Right hand. Right elbow. Right leg. Fingers. Elbow to the face. Kick to the groin. Head butt. Offence.

Offence. Offence. No holding back. She launched herself at him. Always forward. There was no need for defense.

The gunman tried to counter each hit, but he could never recover from the first two surprise blows. This was an attack which he never saw coming from a girl. The two gunmen had miscalculated.

In a flash, Connor came to the realization that Annalise meant that he should take the forward gunman. How did Annalise know that he boxed to keep fit?

"Daniel," he called hoping to shake him out of his paralysis so he'd realize Lenore was unprotected. Daniel instantly pushed Lenore into an alcove and stood with his back to her to keep her safe.

Mobilized by Annalise's energy and the panic flooding his veins with adrenaline, Connor leapt for the remaining gunmen. Pummeling him as fast as he could. Fury replaced the panic with each successful blow. He varied his target from the man's face to his torso, his liver, his kidneys, and back again.

There was a cruelty in the gunman's eyes. It was clear to Connor that this man lived to fight to the death. It was essential for him win this skirmish. Out of nowhere, Jon was suddenly there and instantly felled the forward gunman with a swift strike just below the chin with the palm heel of his hand.

This threw the attacker's head back pinching the nerves at the top of the spinal column. The gunman blacked out. And Jon did it effortlessly without doing all the damage to his hands that Connor now realized was his plight. Talk about one-upmanship.

Jon retrieved cable zip ties from his pants pocket and had the man's hands cuffed behind his back in seconds. Jon looked back. Annalise had pressed her advantage decisively. She'd pinned the second gunman on the floor with her legs squeezing his neck while holding his arm behind his back in a hold both knew was capable of breaking bones. Jon tossed her another zip tie. Connor came to her side to help her to hold the man while she cuffed him.

"Who sent you," Connor demanded still on his adrenaline high. The gunman shrugged making it clear that he wouldn't be talking even if he knew the true answer to that question.

At this point, Brik arrived looking somewhat dazed from being hit by whatever had caused a large gash in his forehead. He was instantly on his communicator calling for backup. He seemed to regret that he didn't have more to contribute.

"Lenore," called Connor. She stepped out from behind Daniel. "Thank you, Daniel."

Daniel nodded. Lenore was visibly shaken. Gone was the courage she and he always gave each other. This fear of physical assault he worried would always stay with her. Connor's girl he feared was permanently scarred by this event. He had protected her for her whole life and now he had let this irreparable damage happen.

Lenore and Connor hugged. "Thank you, my love," she said as she kissed his cheek. The backup guards arrived and removed the prisoners.

Lenore hugged Annalise. "Thank you, Annalise. You saved us. Thank you. You were amazing. I had no idea of this side of you. You were breathtaking."

"Thank you so much for your quick thinking, Annalise," said a grateful Connor. "Are you alright? Will you be alright? "

"Absolutely, Connor. "Better than you I see." She teased nodding at his bloody knuckles. "We're a good team. I'd shake but I suspect it would not be appreciated," she grinned.

"We are all in awe, Annalise," exclaimed an admiring Daniel. "You're going to have to teach me some of those moves," teased Daniel as he and Annalise moved the group forward towards the residential elevator a little worse for wear.

"I think you have far too many moves already" bantered back Annalise about Daniel's endless flirting.

Connor put his arm around Lenore to hold her close as they turned to follow. Lenore whispered in his ear, "I think we should escape through the wormhole as soon as we can."

This caught Connor by surprise for a moment. Of course, she was right. But he'd let himself get attached to these people, their plight, and to his mission to help them.

He stopped for a moment to look at the fear in Lenore's eyes. It turned his stomach. He couldn't remember the last time he'd seen that look. Maybe never. He nodded "Yes" and gave her a comforting smile. They turned to go home.

♦♦♦

The doctor Annalise had sent for Connor's knuckles had been and gone. Dinner had been delivered and eaten. When they were once more finally alone, Lenore turned the TV on loud and motioned Daniel and Connor to a huddle on the couch and coffee table where she hoped they would not be heard.

Lenore spoke quietly under the noise. "Daniel, I know how to work the wormhole. We want to escape. Can you think of a way to break free to get to the wormhole?"

"Lenore, you're incredible. Do you really think we could pull this off?" asked Daniel.

"I think we'll regret it if we don't try," said Lenore.

"What if we staggered our departures and met up en route? What places do we all know?" asked Daniel.

"Just what we see from the window. None of us has been outside," said Lenore.

"Except when we were each brought here," Connor reminded.

"We only travelled along three streets," added Lenore. "Right on Government Avenue to King Street then right to Main Street and left to the station. The wormhole is on Main.

"Maybe it's better just to meet at the station," suggested Daniel.

"Can three of us go in one bubble through the wormhole," wondered Lenore out loud.

"The creatives begin working in groups tomorrow at Breakthru School. Could we use that?" suggested Connor.

"All three of us could leave the room without people noticing. Maybe we could each find a hiding spot in the Complex until its dark," suggested Lenore.

"I know of many hiding spots from that first day of interviews I did which had me recruiting people throughout the Complex. Even in the machine room on the roof," he recalled from meeting Kellin. "That would be a good place for me to hide since I know it. There was no lock on the door."

"You know, this is starting to sound actually do-able," exclaimed Daniel enthusiastically in a hushed voice. "Do you think Annalise would be on our side or theirs? Did you see how she fought to defend us today?" Daniel said incredulously with admiration. "She definitely didn't want anything to happen to us."

Connor considered. "I think it would depend. If we were in danger of being mistreated, I think she'd absolutely be on our side. However, since we're being treated so well, I think she would be on their side. If she thinks we can help, which she says she does, she'll want us here saving her people and her planet."

"Speaking of Kellin," said Daniel, with a light going on. He's the maintenance engineer for the Complex. He would have keys to everywhere. Perhaps we should consider soliciting his help?"

"You and he do have great rapport," reinforced Lenore. "Maybe he would help?"

Connor thought for a moment. "No, I think he'd be like Annalise. He'd want us helping his family and friends to survive. He's very much a family man. A community leader. But if we were in trouble, for sure he'd be there for us.

"He and I trust each other. I wouldn't like to trick him into anything." He stopped himself. "Wait! I just thought of three places to hide. We won't need Kellin's keys." He stopped himself again.

"You know as I think about it, I'm not sure I'd want us to split up. I'd be afraid something might happen to either of you. We can all go to the roof. It has the advantage of letting us see that it's night," said Connor. "It's a low traffic area."

"Then we could use the maintenance elevator. I noticed that there is no camera in it when they brought me up to my suite that way on the gurney," added Lenore.

There was a noise at the suite door. They paused just in case but there was nothing more.

"Do you think they have trackers or microphones planted on us, asked Daniel? Connor shook his head. He then stood up from the couch and put his hand on Daniel's shoulder. "Come on. Let's get some rest, he said parentally above the TV noise. We have a big day tomorrow."

Lenore stood up from sitting on the coffee table and switched off the TV. Daniel waved as he went through the door to the adjoining suite.

"Good night, Daniel," called Lenore.

11
HEROES IN THE MAKING

Connor looked around the lecture amphitheater at the 144 people upon whom the planet was relying for solutions to the crises. He found them heroic in their embrace of their weighty mission despite their trepidations. Every day they had to fight down their insecurities and performance anxieties to try to live up to the expectations of those in power, their loved ones, and indeed all Annutians. They all impressed him.

Recruiting seems to have been very effective despite the speed required and the obstacles to be overcome. A short time-frame. A completely foreign terrain. A society of strict castes and prejudices. Unknown solutions. Only six out of 150 had found the stress too much for them and had asked to be released.

Connor addressed the class. "Good morning, everyone!" Audience members responded in kind. "Over the last few days, you've all been working hard to assimilate a new modus operandi for breakthroughs and creativity that we want you to use to solve the planet's crises.

"School is ending. Our time to begin implementation is at hand. We need to finalize a savant formula for each of you and identify the projects to which you will apply it. Think carefully about your selections as we step through a final review this morning. Let's begin.

"What is a savant formula?"

Sibylla Lund called out, "It's your maximum operation around the application of your strongest most rewarding talents. Your own maximization allows you to merge with the bioflow's maximization process. This enables your capabilities to be extended by those of the bioflow – its evolutionary direction, forces, information, and the capabilities of the living systems it orchestrates. This gives you the means to operate beyond your internal potential."

Sibylla was an unemployed electrical engineer from the shutdown of power plants due to the xenoforming and the switch to fossil fuels. She was referred to his Breakthru Mission by Axl Dahl's wife, Freya. She's a Varunian Freya met through her charity work.

"What else does bioflow integration give you, Sibylla?"

"It's also the means to access spontaneous knowledge as coincidences externally or as breakthroughs and epiphanies internally," continued Sibylla. "The more information fuel you have, the more easily, quickly, and frequently you can re-combine existing information systems to create a novel system or breakthrough that will get you to your goal more quickly.

"One breakthrough could bypass hundreds of steps requisite to achieving a goal. Our goal is to have serial breakthroughs driving our projects. Speed plus invention breakthroughs are of the essence. They are the key thrust of this Breakthru Mission since the normal modi operandi have failed to yield the necessary solutions to our crises. We're a world weak in creativity."

"Sibylla, I like how you've synthesized multiple lectures in a very net way," Connor responded, obviously impressed. "Well done.

"Why did I name your bioflow integration prescription your 'savant formula' and the new modus operandi 'savanting?'"

"It's the best explanation for how savants with no working left brains and thus no ability to access, retain, and process large quantities of data, nevertheless demonstrate that ability," explained Sibylla. "Their access must be external from information databases underlying the bioflow and all of its living information systems including the human species." Connor nodded.

"What is the generic formula for immersing oneself into the bioflow, Dania? Dania Lind suddenly became a deer in headlights. He hadn't meant to catch her off-guard. She had a Ph.D. in astrobiology after all and Sibylla had already given the high-level answer.

Oh. Connor suddenly realized that she was sitting next to Mikael Matsen again, the microbiologist. There was a romance forming between them, so she'd undoubtedly not heard his question.

"Anyone?" asked Connor as he tried to quickly take the spotlight off Dania. "What is the generic formula for immersing oneself into the bioflow?"

Gregor Stinar stood up. He was a lucky find assessed Connor. He'd just graduated top of his class with a master's degree in bioscience engineering and was an expert in environmental technology, rare for his and Annalise's tribe, the Azurites. Gregor had planned to take a year off to travel before settling into a career job. I suspect we wouldn't have acquired him otherwise Connor speculated.

Connor had had to ask Axl to get Azurite Chief of State Einar Nyhus to wine and dine Gregor to impress upon him that his planet needed him. Connor had heard something about a promise of first-class global travel that apparently sealed the deal.

"In its simplest form," began Gregor, "the bioflow is a machinery or set of mechanisms for maximizing living systems for survival. It promotes synergy among living systems. It orchestrates all living systems synchronously into the ideal evolutionary direction for all. Therefore, to integrate into it, one must be moving in the same direction or complying with its goals. One must be operating at one's maximum. Or at least doing activities which will eventually maximize you," Gregor added as an afterthought.

"Maximizing inside means you'll relink with the maximizing machinery outside since they are a single system. When you're complying with the direction and intent of the bioflow, you're letting nature maneuver you into your most advantageous position vis-à-vis other living systems, information, and resources."

"Extremely comprehensive answer, Greg. You're seeing the big picture – how all of the pieces fit together. You're understanding nature's goals and how to exploit them to accelerate your own goals. Thank you for an excellent overview.

"Greg tells us we need to be compliant with our internal maximizing mechanisms to merge with the external maximizing machinery. What then is our maximum?

Dania decided to respond. Connor was pleased that her head was back in the game. She was extremely talented and well-educated. Connor expected great things from her. He wanted to ensure she didn't waste her talents and opportunity for greatness on the distractions of a romance.

"Savantflow. And, before you ask," laughed Dania, "that's the flow state that arises when we're applying our strongest most rewarding talents to the most meaningful and gratifying tasks for an audience that values that work. The biochemistry and electromagnetics of our most desirable emotions, the constellation of our drives for achievement and creation, our maximization instincts and genes have all evolved to pull us to this maximum to ensure the survival of the individual and the species. Savantflow is our automatic mechanism for flicking us into our maximum."

"A very complete answer, Dania. Thank you. So how does one get into savantflow within the bioflow, Dania?"

"Past support from the bioflow is the predictor of its future support. This is because your maximum is a constant and how the bioflow maximizes your system and indeed all living systems is also a constant. Suddenly you can seem to operate as if you have psychic abilities because you know which projects the bioflow will and will not support. Which projects will and will not succeed. Yet it's simply a matter of knowing nature's historical logic, goals, and directions."

"Yes, thank you, Dania," exclaimed Connor enthusiastically. He nodded at her with a proud grin to tell her that she had redeemed herself. "How does one discover one's savant formula?"

Olivia Ohlson stood up. She and Kellin's son Rolland were the youngest of the creatives at age 20. "To identify one's savant formula, we simply need to look at our past pattern of events and activities that launched our savantflows.

"Whatever the theme of the activities causing our savantflows was in the past – our *savantflows theme* – will predict how you can move into savantflow in the future. Your *savantflows theme* will be your *savant formula* for moving into future savantflows.

"Or, uh, I guess you could call it your *savantflow-bioflow theme*. It's this theme which will tell each of us precisely which projects to choose for success with Annutia's Breakthru Mission.

"Right you are, Olivia," confirmed Connor to validate both to Liv and the group that he respected how talented she was. She was another KahlDahr like Kellin and Rolland who was brilliant and inventive despite having been deprived of a formal education.

"*Savantflow-bioflow theme* captures our goal perfectly, doesn't it? Thank you, Olivia." Connor was pleased that he'd been right about Liv. Despite being so young she was excelling at savanting.

He had recruited her from the Programming Department after recruiting Kellin. Like Kellin, Liv had been overlooked as all KahlDahr are. Their protruding brows make them appear both menacing and primitive. Also, she was female, beautiful, poor, confident, creative, and self-educated, all of which increased the discrimination she had endured over her short life.

The ruling castes had missed that, with Liv's unity consciousness, she could see how massive computer systems fit together. She had an executive perspective. Yet she could also work brilliantly on all the tiny details composing that larger picture.

He and Annalise had been waiting for the elevator for the Council Chamber when he watched her flowchart all of the systems for a bullying, condescending executive. He was obviously very much her senior, yet he was having great difficulty grasping the breadth of her thinking.

"What if you can't identify the pattern in your past savantflow events. How else might you determine your savant formula?"

"Your *spontaneous-knowledge theme*," called someone from the audience but Connor couldn't see whom it was. "Determine the theme of the activities you were doing when you experienced breakthroughs, epiphanies, coincidences and other spontaneous knowledge events.

"Exactly," said Connor. Other ways of determining your savant formula?

Kellin stood up, "Your *unpaid-work theme*. This entails an examination of the events in your past when you've done work that you crave so much that you'd do it for free. You love it that much. Whereas, others would charge for it because they consider it work. You should be able to trace this theme in patterns of events in your past.

"You'll have emotional highs when you're doing this kind of work so the *positive-emotions theme* will also apply. When you do it, there'll also be the expected occurrences of spontaneous knowledge, flashes of genius, breakthroughs, and clusters of coincidences.

"This is exactly right, Kellin. You've lived your savant formula, haven't you – since you made the car that died on your front lawn operational in your pre-teen years." Kellin nodded.

"What's the difference between breakthroughs, coincidences, spontaneous knowledge and epiphanies," Connor continued.

Kellin, still standing, responded. "Nothing. They're all re-combinations of information systems inside of you or outside of you to invent a new information system. They're all part of the larger scheme of the creative evolutionary advance of the bioflow. Nature can't always solve evolutionary challenges in a gradual incremental way. It must use quantum leaps to create a human eye for example. We want to harness the bioflow's creativity production line to solve the crises of our world."

"Excellent, Kellin," Connor beamed. I never specifically stated that they were all part of the same continuum that connects our inner systems and brain to the bioflow or that they are simply an extension of nature's own universal creative, adaptive, evolutionary process, but you figured it out.

"You're obviously going to excel at exploiting the bioflow for your projects, Kellin. Just as you see how the systems of this huge Government Complex run, you have the expanded consciousness to grasp how the systems of the universe interconnect and operate."

Connor wanted to ensure that KahlDahr Kellin, Rolland, Olivia and others were not intimidated by those with multiple degrees or from more elevated castes. He wanted them free to create and achieve at the maximum of their significant talents.

Connor was a big Kellin fan. The KahlDahr was so incredibly talented. He was also good people. The two had a special bond. They both shared a wisdom that comes from living from unity consciousness and seeing how everything is connected, even the two of them. He had a warm spot in his heart for Olivia and Kellin's son, Rolland, for the same reason.

Rolland was still working on his biology degree, yet his expansive brilliance was more insightful than mature professionals in that field. He could see biological systems as ingeniously as his father could see mechanical systems or Liv could see programming systems. All three had effortlessly absorbed the systems thinking underlying savanting.

"You've created a quantum leap for everyone, Kellin. In savantflow, your concentration is simply on the creative act you are doing. You become pure creation. This is our natural state. This is nature's natural state. This is my process of savanting in a nutshell.

"Let's say you've never been free during your life to discover your unpaid work theme. What other patterns of events in your past could you track to determine your savant formula?" No one responded. "How else could you get into savantflow within the bioflow?" No one responded. "What other themes could you follow?" No one responded.

He had told them that all of the themes point to the same savant formula, so perhaps they thought learning only one or two would be enough. However, being fluent in them all means that you'll be able to action incoming events in your life more quickly. You'll make directional decisions faster.

"We've identified the *savantflows theme* or *savantflow-bioflow theme*, the *spontaneous-*

knowledge theme, the *unpaid-work theme*, and the *positive-emotions theme*. What else?"

Finally, Henerik Halderson posited an answer. "You can look at the events of new knowledge that you naturally pursued since childhood."

When they recruited him, Henerik was a biochemistry degree dropout seeking to find himself and his purpose. Henerik had blossomed with the Breakthru Mission and School. He had found his purpose.

"Yes, good," reinforced Connor. "You want to assess the common thread of any new learning that you voluntarily sought. Your *learning-pursuit theme* or *knowledge-pursuit theme*.

Henerik nodded before continuing, "What growth have you sought historically? Your *growth theme* or *growth-pursuit theme*. What is the theme that runs through the times in your past when you were creative or inventive? And what is the common territory of new creations that you've historically sought? Your *creativity theme* or *creation theme*? Also, in what fields did you choose to be creative? What is your *creativity-pursuit theme*?

"And what is the commonality of the new territories of knowledge or new frontiers that you've historically penetrated? Your *frontier-pursuit theme*. These are all likely to also generate emotional highs so, as Kellin indicated, you could also track what work or activities generated passion, excitement, and enthusiasm. Your *positive-emotions theme*."

"Good work, Henerik! You've added a number of categories of past events to our list for assessment. There are a couple more that offer alternative means to identify your savant formula. Anyone? Yes, Marta."

Marta Kaase was a Varunian electrical engineer also laid off from the power plants like fellow-Varunian Sibylla. Connor had learned that in the Annutia caste system, Varunians were one step above the KahlDahr and one rung below the Azurites.

"Your *successful-projects theme*," suggested Marta. "I think we could pick our future projects based on our past successful projects – ones with the tell-tale arrows that everyone has been identifying."

"You're exactly right, Marta. When you're choosing your projects for the Breakthru Mission, you'll want to ensure you capitalize on the formula that has created successful projects in your past. Now that you know about the bioflow, you don't want to see those projects as isolated events. There is a pattern. If you can dig for it, there is no need to ever pursue a project that will not succeed again. Never again will you swim upstream against the bioflow to try to make a project work.

"We know if it's a right project for us that we will see clusters of coincidences, breakthroughs and other spontaneous knowledge events, facilitating events and gates, emotional highs, and serial savantflows. Marta, what will we see if we choose projects not on the yellow-brick road, so to speak?"

"Blocks," said Marta. "Setbacks. Negative emotions. The absence of any arrows or signposts. Hard work step-by-step instead of coincidences and facilitating events catapulting you forward hundreds of steps at a time.

"You'll have to use discipline to push yourself to keep going instead of being pulled forward by compelling drives. The formula of past failed projects will continue in the future. There is now a predictability that never existed for me before. There appears to be an incredible order to reality where we assumed chaos."

"Precisely," said Connor. "Well done, Marta. I've asked you all to start developing hypotheses as to what projects you want to pursue to solve the planet's crises. When you test them out, if they're wrong for you or the planet or the evolutionary bioflow of the planet, Marta has described precisely what you'll experience. You'll then need to quickly replace those projects.

"We can do your first test right now. When you think of doing the project you have selected, are you excited or does your energy nosedive? That is your first indication. Are you going to have to push yourself to do the wrong project rather than being joyfully excited by the right project? Excellent work, Marta."

"Who has remembered the last two themes or patterns of past events that you can evaluate?" probed Connor further.

Sven Steensen called out, "Your historical meaning theme or *meaning-pursuit theme*. What projects, work, or contributions have historically given your life meaning. What contributions do you crave to make?"

Sven was a mechanical engineer. Like Sibylla Lund and Marta Kaase, he was also laid off from a hydropower company as they had to return to burning fossil fuels.

"Thank you, Sven. Obviously, we need everyone doing work that is meaningful to them. This is part of the positive-emotions theme when you're on the right path to maximization and immersion into the bioflow.

What is the last theme to identify one's savant formula? Jordaan, what is the one we're missing? The most elusive one until you develop this skill?"

"Resonance. Your pattern or *theme of resonance events*," exclaimed Jordaan Jostad after a moment of pensive reflection. An astrophysicist, Jordaan is adept at applying the laws of physics and chemistry to explain the birth, life and death of stars, planets, galaxies, nebulae and other objects in the universe.

This was the perfect direction for someone who'd been addicted to the pursuit of astronomy and cosmology since his childhood years with his Dad, a world-renowned astronomer. Much to his surprise, his Dad was all in favor of Jordaan participating in the Breakthru Mission. Connor learned why at a social event at Axl's home.

Apparently, Dad attributes his own success to an incredible memory and the logic to apply that knowledge. While they were both passionate about the same fields, these were not Jordaan's strengths. He showed signs of being much more inventive, imaginative, and creative. Jordaan had a gift for inventing new scientific equipment and designing unprecedented computer software to analyze data and such. Dad's strengths were left-brain; his son's were right-brain.

Dad had realized when Connor selected his son that he'd recruited the right strengths for the Annutia Breakthru Mission. He felt Commander Kane could teach Jordaan things that he could not. That Kane could cultivate in his son strengths that he himself did not possess.

Because Jostad Sr, believed so much in Connor, he had secured additional funding for the program to ensure its success. Connor was pleased to have a creative as talented as Jordaan in the group.

"You are exactly right," confirmed Connor. "Tell us about resonance and how to use it, Jordaan."

"This is our frequency-sensing ability. You are one tuning fork. When you concentrate on a direction option which is the right one to take towards maximization within the maximization direction of the bioflow, it's like a second tuning fork starts to tone in resonance with you, the first tuning fork. This is how you can proceed quickly and safely into unknown territory.

"You look at your list of possible directions and choose the one where you feel the surge of a second tuning beginning to cause vibration within you in resonance."

"Is resonance the same as gut feel or intuition, Jordaan?

"No, sir. It has no additional information other than two things having the same frequency."

"Precisely. Well done. Thank you, Jordaan." Connor went to turn away and then turned back to ask as an afterthought, "Have you ever used your resonance, Jordaan?"

"No, sir."

"Raise your hands. Who has used resonance or thinks they have? About 20%. I suspect that within a couple of months, most of you will raise your hands. Resonance or frequency-sensing is faster in determining direction. It means you won't have to test various direction hypotheses to look for other indicator events in your reality before you can determine your best direction in which to proceed.

"Now, what if you don't have the patterns of events of any of these themes in your past. A *no-themes* situation. What does that mean? What should you do? Yes, Mikael?"

"This means you've lived your life directed by external elements – you've been externally referenced – rather than complying with your natural addictive drives internally – or been internally referenced. Consequently, you haven't maximized. Therefore, you haven't merged with the bioflow. As a result, you'll have less consistent patterns or fewer of them to help you to determine direction to achieve your goals. You won't be able to recruit the power of the bioflow."

Connor was pleased that Mikael had taken his attention off Dania long enough to participate. Mikael was brilliantly creative, perhaps the best after Kellin. Connor knew when he recruited him that he was going to excel at using savanting to solve the crises. Since then he'd proven even better than expected.

Mikael was another brilliant Varunian bench-pressing out of his caste. That he should have had difficulty finding work was such a waste of extraordinary talent. Connor was grateful for his availability to contribute to the Breakthru Mission.

"So, what do you need to do, Mikael?"

"Start savanting with serial savantflows so that the indicators will emerge. Then you can use them to predict your future and your ideal direction."

"Exactly, Mikael. However, I'll give you all a hint. None of you are in this 'no-themes' category. You were recruited based on your themes of past events in your life and their match to the planetary crises.

"Good work, everyone!" Connor praised. I'm going to give you the rest of today to analyze your past patterns of events to help you to pick out at least one project that has the greatest chance of success. Know your savant formula. Then use that formula to select the projects that you would be most excited to pursue to save Annutia."

12
DANIEL'S ESCAPE

"Okay, back to the residences," said Connor to conclude a long day of the creatives working on their projects. "Relax and enjoy your evening. Get some rest. We'll begin again tomorrow." The creatives began milling around to chat as they slowly began to gather into groups for a protected walk back to the residences with bodyguards.

Connor and Lenore gathered with Annalise, Brik and Jon to return to their home suite.

"Where is Daniel," asked Annalise?

"I have no idea," shrugged Connor.

"Me neither," said Lenore. "Do you think he went back to the residences with the students?"

Annalise called over to Niels to see if that was the case.

"Niels hasn't seen him."

Annalise was on the phone again. "I need all available agents to scan the building for visiting dignitary, Daniel Lowe.

During the silence, Olivia motioned Connor aside. "May I speak to you a moment, Commander?"

"Of course, Liv. What's on your mind?"

"Do you remember where you found me in Programming Room C filled with about 200 programmers?" She asked in a hushed voice while continuing to pressure him to separate from everyone else.

"I do," said Connor.

"There are four such rooms next to each other, A, B, C, D. You may have noticed that there is no security required to enter these rooms because they are open resources for inhouse work and for visitors. At the back of each room are two disposal tubes, one for paper waste and one for other waste. On a darc, a bunch of us went down the paper tube to see where it went.

"It goes to a room where the paper is packaged up for recycling. It was a fun ride. It ends right next to the freight elevator exit. Anyone could easily exit the Government Complex there without cameras or security.

"If you were ever to travel about the city, I would hope you would visit me in Pihl district. I have a house in my name, so I should be easy to find. You, Lenore and Daniel have an open invitation.

"Kellin and Rolland Bergh live a block away. I'm certain they would love to join in on any social events. Both of us have spare rooms for the three of you whenever you would like. Connor looked over at Kellin. Both Kellin and Rolland were watching Olivia talk to Connor. Kellin nodded to confirm what Olivia was saying.

"How kind of you, Liv. We'd be delighted. We're going to try to make that happen at the earliest possible opportunity." He could see that Olivia was reading between the lines just as he had read the meaning in her offer as well.

Olivia took the opportunity to shake Connor's hand to put something in it which he instinctively pocketed post-handshake. Later, Connor discovered the personal cards of both Olivia and Kellin with their addresses and contact information. There was a hand-drawn map on the back of Kellin's card.

"Wonderful," said Liv graciously as the squawking of Jon's walkie talkie broke up their conversation.

"We've found Daniel Lowe. He was locked on the roof. We'll bring him to you."

Three burly uniformed guards brought an embarrassed Daniel back to the entourage waiting in the lecture hall.

Daniel sheepishly shrugged, "I just wanted some fresh air and to see the view. Unfortunately, the door locked behind me. I had no phone."

"Whatever possessed you, Daniel," admonished Lenore selling the lie as cool as a cucumber. As usual. "You gave us such a fright. Don't do that again."

"Believe me, I won't," Daniel assured them with feigned earnestness.

♦♦♦

When they got back to the suite, Connor flicked on the TV loud. Connor said in a hushed voice, "Obviously, the roof is out as a staging area for us to await darkness. Thank goodness you found out about the lock, Daniel. We could've all been stuck up there when we had already committed to our escape."

"You know, you could've told us," complained Lenore.

"It wasn't planned. But my resonance was strong that I had to do it. I saw an opportunity when no one was looking and just took it," Daniel confessed. "I thought I'd be back in a minute or two with no one the wiser."

"Olivia has given us another option. Really Liv and Kellin. I've a feeling they've figured out that we're prisoners and have laid out a route for our escape." Connor explained the details to them. "I'm certain that Liv has no idea about our plans to try for the wormhole."

Lenore surprised them with another alternative. "There's an air conditioning duct between our bedroom and that of the empty suite next door. I'm small enough to make it through. I tested it out in my suite on the lower floor. If they hadn't arranged a call between the two of us, Connor, I'd have been gone that night."

"I could then open the adjoining door for you both to pass through. When the time is right we could then exit through that suite. The door to that neighboring suite is right across from the stairs. The turns in the hallway hide the exit from that suite from the guards in front of our suite."

"Great," said Daniel, "We now have an option to leave from here or the Government West Tower depending on when the opportunity arises."

13
EMANCIPATION

"We've thrown a lot at you over the last few weeks," began Connor. "We've asked you to put your lives on hold. To learn a new way of operating. To put aside your fears for your survival and the survival of your family and friends. To fight a different kind of war differently. To apply all your talents and skills to do what may be the most important work of your life. Saving your planet and your people. We're extremely grateful for your sacrifice.

"As we walked around the room to spend time trying to accelerate each of your projects, there are a few items that have come to our attention that I'd like to address today and tomorrow. Your emancipation, execution creatives, and protecting yourself and your work.

"When we talk about your savant formula or your savant domain, I want to emphasize that we're not trying to assign you to a box. Nature routinely determines your ideal path within the bioflow. But the bioflow is forever adapting. Advances in one living system changes the context of another system causing the second system to have to adapt, which changes the context again, so other systems must adapt, and so on and so on as the dance continues. The box is dynamic not constant.

"But more than this we need to undo the damage preventing you from this adaptation in the bioflow. We need to free you to be internally referenced as Mikael described for those in the no-themes category. Many of you have experienced persecution or discrimination for which your quality of life and even your survival required you to be continuously externally referenced and hyper-vigilant.

"We don't want to suggest a throwback to Ayn Rand's 1938 dystopian novella, *Anthem*. Connor raised his hand. Does anyone know this story? Most shook their heads.

Someone called out, "1938 is a little before our time." Laughter from the audience.

Connor smiled and nodded in understanding. "For me too, I'll have you know." He bantered back with feigned indignation. More laughter.

"Well, Rand created a collectivism civilization in which the people have no personal freedom and live only to serve their state. The concepts of individuality, achievement, thinking, creating, and experimenting had been eradicated.

"A Council of Vocations assigns each person to a job when they come of age. Each person's vocation is supposedly a way in which the society can use his or her talents effectively and for the benefit of everyone. Much as the Breakthru Mission hopes to spawn.

"Each person must go to that job until s/he is forty years old. Then they must retire to the Home of the Useless." Laughter from the audience. "They assign Equality 7-2521, the 21-year-old male protagonist, to be a Street Sweeper despite his yearning to be a Scholar.

"As Rand's story unfolds, we share in his rebellion against this collective, totalitarian society in order to find himself. With delightful understatement and matter-of-factness, Rand demonstrates the way that collectivism destroys man's instinct to better himself and his people.

"Then our rebel hero breaks all the laws and rules of conduct in order to make a great gift to all of mankind. The rediscovery of electricity and the lightbulb. His great gift was immediately rejected by the World Council of Scholars which he wanted to join because it would be disastrous for the Department of Candles." Laughter.

"But also because the Scholars were outraged by the arrogance of Equality 7-2521 in thinking a Street

Sweeper and an individual had the right to discover something outside of a collective. Accordingly, they decide he must die. Equality 7-2521 grabs his lightbox creation and runs for dear life.

"In his new home far away, Equality 7-2521 discovers, in a library of old books, the meaning of the forbidden word 'I' in a world where only 'we' had been allowed. As his 'I' identity grows, he changes his name to Prometheus, the giver of the knowledge of fire to humankind in Greek mythology. After all, he was the giver of the electric light.

"He decides to establish a new world based on free thinking and respect for the individual. He wants to launch an age of technological innovation. Prometheus swears that he'll free all the enslaved. He discovers another forbidden word which he takes as the heart of the meaning and the glory of his new world. 'Ego.'

"Rand's anthem is that 'ego' is the prioritizing of one's own interests. One's dedication should be more to oneself than to the collective, and that one is the proper beneficiary of one's actions. Rand's ideal is for self-sufficiency and self-motivated accomplishment.

"As with Equality 7-2521, many of you have been assigned work by Annutian society based on your castes or upbringing or past bad behavior as in Rand's *Anthem* world. Many of you have been prevented from doing the work that would not only be truly rewarding for you, but which would allow you to contribute the most to the world. It's time to not only remove these shackles but all memory of them. This is the moment of your emancipation. Can you feel it?

"What I'm proposing is total freedom from these societally defined work assignments. Release to your natural state since birth. Capitalize on nature's intelligence, knowledge, organizing principles, resources, and evolutionary direction with which we have evolved to operate symbiotically, synergistically, and synchronistically.

"Despite the pressure of Annutia's crises in the Breakthru Mission, the only one deciding your ideal job must be nature's bioflow. All Lenore, Daniel, Annalise, and I will be doing is helping you to decipher nature's instructions.

"We want you all to release from the shackles of prejudice and societal constraints that have confined your lives. We want you to discover freedom as Equality 7-2521 did. The time has come to throw off the chains of a jailor society which you must now save.

"Making a contribution to the State does not need to be dictated as in *Anthem*. It is innate. We receive the greatest gratification biochemically and electromagnetically when what we do contributes to the maximization and success of the species. How could a successful human species have biologically evolved otherwise?

"Nature's bioflow which orchestrates and co-evolves all living systems is committed to the survival of living systems advantageous to the whole. This means that mechanisms inside and outside of us have evolved to favor your individual maximization and the contribution of each individual to the maximization of the human species as a whole.

"When you're doing the work that maximizes you, then this work will automatically be work that is helping to maximize the human species. It is built-in. If you were nature, you would organize logically in this way as well. For those of you who couldn't freely follow your passions up to this point, I would like you to rewrite your past lives in order to rewrite the people you are now.

"People thought of Bill Gates as someone who was only interested in making money. However, it was because of his focus on helping people across the world, that he made the money. His family was very community-minded and deeply committed to charitable works. It was this childhood theme that inspired Microsoft and all the creative thinking about how to make people successful and impactful that became hallmarks of Gates success.

"People were surprised when Gates left the money-making machine of Microsoft for mega-philanthropy. They missed that this was a better way for him to continue with his childhood life theme.

"Because Gates had been serially in savantflows his whole life and thus continuously attached to the bioflow, he had always been orchestrated to contributing to the advance of the species. In fact, orchestration by the bioflow is how he was always ahead of evolving markets.

"Society had simply missed the theme of his creative acts. Especially those who had come to see money as the root of all evil and judged all those with money negatively. Their prejudice had misread the magnanimity of the man.

"The pursuit of a savant domain career is your human right. It will become the future right of a smarter Annutian society which prioritizes the maximization of the planet's human resources for the benefit of all – regardless of race, religion, sex, age, wealth, poverty, or any of the many discriminations that have caused society to discard talent and impede contribution.

"Similarly, the ultimate corporate competitive advantage will become the maximization of all employees in their savant domains, all working to the benefit of the company. State-of-the-art recruiting and talent management will change drastically as a result.

"Today, you finalize your projects to resolve Annutia's crises. Tomorrow, you'll take your hypothesis of whatever projects will use your strengths to the maximum and test them out. Does the bioflow support or oppose? Test hypothesis after hypothesis until you find the one with the best bioflow support.

"Who has not figured out their first project?" Connor scanned the raised hands in the room. "About 15%. Good work for the other 85%. Okay, let's work together as a group to get this last 15% ready for action on a project tomorrow. "Since Lenore, Daniel, Annalise, and I are only four people, I wonder if the rest of you could join in groups of two or more to help the 15%.

"Why don't we each take a row along the left wall so the 15% can find us. Then let's brainstorm until everyone has their project ready for tomorrow. You will all gain benefit for your own work by seeing how the bioflow has been operating in the lives of others. The opportunity to practice reading patterns will speed your project going forward.

"For the 15%, once you have your answer, please sign up under one of the various categories of projects on the front board or create a new category. We can then ensure that we have enough seating and tables for each category tomorrow.

"We think meeting with others in your category will generate mutual support, synergy, synchronization, and better differentiation of your projects within your shared fields. Okay. Let's get creative," encouraged Connor as he, Lenore, Annalise, and Daniel each took a seat in the first four rows on the left wall.

14

EXECUTION CREATIVES

As Connor and his entourage entered the noisy auditorium, the creatives quickly assumed their seats. "This is an exciting day," announced Connor with a gleam in his eye. "Today is the formal project launch!" he exclaimed excitedly. "Our war on the invading xenoformers begins today!" "Hurrahs" from the audience erupted. When the uproar subsided, Connor continued.

"There are a few final items for me to share before we begin: protecting yourselves and your projects plus accelerating them through execution creativity. "First, a moment on your physical security. Some of you have thought it a game to ditch your bodyguards.

"You may not be aware that Lenore, Daniel, Annalise, and I were attacked a few days ago in the concourse by a team hoping to kidnap us or worse. Without the heroic efforts of Annalise, Brik and Jon, we would no longer be with you." Connor waved to the right of the stage where all three were sitting with

Lenore and Daniel. As the audience began to clap, Connor joined in.

"As you each develop breakthroughs in providing water, power, the means to fight the xenoforming, and so on, you'll become more valuable than we are. If you value your lives and value your contributions to the world, then please value your bodyguards and the security guards we've assign to your work areas. They are not superfluous. They must become part of your new lives going forward. Embrace them, please. Respect them.

"Now let's move on to talk about protecting your inventions. This needs to start today," advised Connor. "In ordinary times, the kinds of breakthroughs you're likely to generate would be at risk for theft, corporate espionage, attack, and interference from all sorts of competitors and power players. However, as Annutia faces increasingly more dire challenges, the interest in what you develop is going to become even more compelling.

"The provision of water, for example. We're talking about survival here. Powerful people will be using all of their resources to ensure their own survival and even their dominance. You need to protect what you invent.

"In addition, with lives at stake, you'll feel enormous pressure to complete solutions to the threats to the survival of your people and your planet. As a result, you'll be tempted to ignore my warnings to put time into protecting your inventions as you go. However, again, people will become more and more desperate as the threats to survival increase.

"What you create to benefit all of mankind may be stolen for financial gain or so that a few may use it to dominate others. This will exacerbate the crises. Lives will be lost because you didn't protect the fruits of your creativity. Please take to heart the precautions with which we have been attempting to arm you.

"Thanks to our generous benefactor Minister Plenipotentiary Axl Dahl, Dahl Enterprises will source any funding that you need through venture capitalists, investment bankers, dealmakers, and partners. We'll have lawyers of every kind available to make you successful.

"We'll have intellectual property lawyers to protect your creations and to ensure you aren't encroaching on the intellectual property of others. We'll have contract lawyers to negotiate your best deals. We'll have litigation lawyers if you get into trouble. You'll have business advisors and other resources as you need them.

"To help you document every step of your invention process in case of lawsuits, we're providing each project with three video cameras. One pointed at your computer. One pointed into your work space and one to go with you everywhere.

"Label what is on each tape. Then it will be effortless to provide the proof to prevent any legal cases without distracting you from your critical work. We want the lawyers in a position to quickly quash any legal battles in court on your behalf as soon as they arise.

"We'll also be providing offline computers with advanced encryption, and even a vault to protect what you create. It will include safety deposit boxes of all sizes for which only you will have the keys. Cots and sleeping bags, meals etc. will be made available here as necessary because nothing of your work should go back to the residences. We can't provide the same level of protection there. Enough said.

"Now I want to talk about *execution creatives* who can accelerate your projects. Execution talent is also a form of creativity. We recruited some of you because you can implement anything in any field faster than even experts in those fields. This is because you intuitively partner with the bioflow to court coincidences and fuel breakthroughs to catapult you ahead. Somehow you see the gates and pathways that are open for accelerating projects.

"By using your gift for execution, you achieve the same speed whether moving into known or unknown territory. You are execution geniuses and we suspect you were execution child prodigies. But, more than a talent for implementation, you have a passion for it.

Put your hands up if you are an achievement junkie. Keep them up please.

"Everyone, please take note of these execution savants so you can recruit them for your projects. As your partnership with the bioflow solidifies, you will all become execution creatives. However, during the crises when time is short, you owe it to yourself and the planet to have all the help available. Entice these execution creatives to work on your projects to accelerate your progress and to teach you how they do what they do.

"Before you take your hands down, execution creatives, I want you to notice that you are the 15% who did not have projects. You did not fail the mission or the planet. We specifically recruited you because you were execution creatives.

You are the grease that can make all of the other projects work. Find the projects you want to accelerate. It is the execution creatives who will change the world. They already have. Let me demonstrate.

"I want to talk about the famous Earth entrepreneurs you studied at school, the founders of Microsoft, Facebook, Blackberry, Amazon, Apple, and Google. They all reinforce the need to protect your inventions since they had to deal with those trying to cash in on their financial success. Therefore, it's a given that the same will happen to you should you too become successful. However, I've brought them up for another reason.

"The real strengths of the founders of these companies was in their *execution creativity* – rather than some single brilliant idea upon which each company was founded. Their founders were *execution creatives*. This is the key to their success.

"Amazon was not the first online retailer. It was simply the best due to hundreds of daily innovations and adaptations that are a way of life for its creative culture. Founder Jeff Bezos has created a company which adapts, innovates, experiments, fails and corrects, diversifies, and expands faster than its competitors.

"Facebook was not the first social network. It had the best initial and ongoing execution. It is more in touch with its community base, more reactive to their needs, and more protecting of personal information and privacy.

It has not only kept pace with the continual advancements in its field but has increasingly originated them just as Amazon has. Founder Mark Zuckerberg created an environment of unbridled innovation and execution creativity right from the start.

"You all know I'm a movie fan," grinned Connor. "I so enjoy the line in the hit 2010 movie, *The Social Network*, about the founding of Facebook where

Zuckerberg says of the Winklevosses, '*If you guys were the inventors of Facebook, you'd have invented Facebook.*'

"Zuckerberg brings home my point regarding execution finesse by saying, '*You have part of my attention - you have the minimum amount. The rest of my attention is back at the offices of Facebook, where my colleagues and I are doing things that no one in this room, including and especially your clients, are intellectually or creatively capable of doing.*'

"The Winklevoss twins expected that their one social network idea – that was not even implemented for Facebook and was not even original – entitled them to earn the profits that were generated by the thousands of events of innovation, adaptation, and execution creativity that Zuckerberg, his friends, and his team had to do daily to create and advance Facebook to the success that it is today.

"On Earth, we changed all intellectual property laws to favor execution not ideas. Just as with trademarks, patents now also face a 'use it or lose it' proposition. There is no coming back after decades of successful implementation to snipe the profits of the execution creatives responsible such as in the BlackBerry story. Especially when the patent owners have demonstrated no ability to implement themselves.

"I encourage you to think beyond your inventions to implementation. Court coincidences and creativity in that part of your projects too in partnership with the bioflow. Also, the method of execution may require you to modify your inventions.

"Lenore, Daniel, Annalise, and I are all adept execution creatives. We're good implementers because we're always exploiting the bioflow. Its resources, for sure. But more importantly, its direction of evolution. Please call on us if you think we can help. We can even generate project plans based on your individual history of support from the bioflow.

"Former Supreme Commander, Axl Dahl, will be coming tomorrow to update us on the state of the crises and to answer your questions. He may be bringing other council members as well so think of what you would like to know to better target or speed your projects.

"Okay. Breakthru School's out for today. Go do your magic on the Breakthru Mission. Good luck, everyone!"

15

AXL'S UPDATE

Connor, Lenore, Annalise, and Daniel were circulating around to help at the tables set aside in the ballroom for the various project groups. Everyone paused when Axl Dahl entered the front of the ballroom with Defense Minister Karsten Kolbeck, in tow. Both ministers looked seriously strained.

Four large military officers followed them in. The way they spread out and cased the room suggested they were security agents protecting the Ministers. Brik and Jon connected up with the most senior officer and spoke deferentially in quiet whispers. They then moved closer to Connor, Lenore, Daniel and Annalise now congregating at the front of the lecture hall. They whispered to Annalise. She immediately looked at Axl with great concern.

Connor took the microphone at the front of the hall. "Creatives, I am pleased to welcome the Minister Plenipotentiary Axl Dahl who is a key benefactor for your work through his Dahl Enterprises." The creatives clapped appreciatively.

"In addition, it is my pleasure to introduce Defense Minister Karsten Kolbeck." Additional clapping. "Gentlemen, welcome. The floor is yours." Connor stepped to the side of the stage to sit with Lenore.

Daniel, as usual, had been standing near Annalise when Brik and Jon had been whispering to her. As inconspicuously as possible, he gradually sauntered over to where Connor and Lenore were sitting.

He leaned in and whispered, "There have been three attempts on Axl's life including a shooting."

Connor and Lenore looked aghast at the thought of losing a fond friend. A moment later they contemplated the repercussions on their own lives, their work, and their return to Earth. Their own safety was now an issue as they felt the weight of abandonment at the thought of losing Axl.

If Axl's enemies would kill him to stop the Breakthru Mission, they would certainly kill his three facilitators. They wondered if it was the warmongers, the smart drug manufacturers, or some other power players that Connor had suspected were pulling the strings of puppet leader, Supreme Commander Riis.

Lenore leaned in and whispered, "We'd better escape through the wormhole tonight. We're more at risk than we thought. Connor felt torn since he found the Breakthru Mission irresistible and he was on the verge of launching the world changers – the world savers – to do their magic.

According to the savanting process he had developed, he shouldn't feel conflicted if fleeing tonight was the right thing to do or the timing was right for the bioflow. He decided he had better watch for some flow events before he should agree.

Then Connor looked deeply into Lenore's eyes. He saw the fear. He succumbed to his weakness for protecting her. He chose to overrule his resonance and nodded his agreement.

"I understand that most of you will be addressing the following crises," Axl began. "The water shortage, the power shortage, arresting the xenoforming, reversing the xenoforming, capitalizing on the xenoforming, the latter being one person's ambition that I find personally appealing, he said with an enthusiastic smile. Who was that?"

"Father and son, Kellin and Rolland Bergh, Minister Dahl," said Kellin as they both stood up.

"Very good," nodded Axl.

They nodded back at him as they sat down. Connor immediately identified this exchange as a flow event demonstrating support from the bioflow for this mission.

Axl continued his list. "And finally, off-world colonization should we not be able to save Annutia –

full terraforming or para-terraforming under a dome on other planets, our two moons, an asteroid, or a space station.

"There are a few more territories I would like you to consider for those who haven't yet identified your ideal project. You've been protected from the distraction of what has been going on in our world while you were going through your intensive training. Circumstances have grown critical. So, I now want to bring you up to date and ensure you're kept up to date in the fields of your respective projects from here on in.

"The most important of recent events haven't yet been revealed to the public. Therefore, I must remind you to honor your confidentiality agreements with respect to what I reveal next. We now have feedback from our reconnaissance missions along the wormhole to find the invaders who are xenoforming our planet."

Videos of the invader's planet from the reconnaissance mission began playing on the large screen behind Axl. "The inhabitants live in spacesuits underground near the center of a metropolis." Audience members gasped at the barren devastation and the first sight of an actual threat to their existence.

"We know who they are and where their home planet is," continued Axl. Given the state of their planet and the xenoforming on ours, we've decided to name their planet Miasma after a contagious power that has an independent life of its own found in Greek mythology. Miasma means dangerous, foreboding, or deathlike influence or atmosphere.

"The enemy inhabitants may or may not be humanoid. They've only been seen in spacesuits, so we're not sure what they look like. They've built structures and domiciles all over their planet. However, most seem to be vacant. The population seems to have congregated in the large central structures which seem to be connected by a web of underground concourses. We suspect that some sort of crisis is causing them to centralize underground.

"We assume they need the algae for food and their gas emissions for respiration. We suspect they might also need water for themselves and the algae but Miasma is without it – at least that we can see on the surface.

Our scientists have noted that many of the vacated structures follow dried river beds, lakes and even along the shores of what could be considered oceans. This suggests that Miasma is facing a water crisis. Further investigation has yielded an atmosphere of catastrophically high carbon dioxide content.

"Our computer simulation shows that a large increase in atmospheric carbon dioxide can cause a loss of planetary water. The result would be a barren landscape such as was observed. A planet can lose its water to the atmosphere and then to space due to an increase in greenhouse gases like carbon dioxide.

"Greenhouse gases trap heat within the planet's atmosphere. Water evaporation from oceans into the atmosphere accelerates as surface temperatures rise to 135°F. The Miasmians seem to have triggered a runaway greenhouse effect. Unfortunately, experimentation with the simulation couldn't show that the situation could be reversed – even by massively removing the excess carbon dioxide.

"Our reconnaissance scientists saw fossilizations of the same algae that we now have living on our lakes and rivers. If these beings need the gases from the algae and perhaps it is also their food, then they must be dying without them. This would lead them to xenoform our planet.

"Alternatively, their attack could simply be an act of war. They can wipe us out with the algae cocktail without any loss of life on their part. How could we defend ourselves? Or how could we go on the offensive with the limited information we have available to us?

"A third alternative hypothesis posits that the algae escaped the dying Miasma planet unaided through the wormhole in search of greener pastures, so to speak. Then, what we see on Miasma could become Annutia's fate. We would be their encore."

Video images of the crises on Annutia began to play on the screen behind Minister Dahl. Gasps and other guttural reactions spread through the ballroom. The fear was palpable. There was devastation; conflicts; long lineups for food and water; hunger and thirst on faces; refugees covered in dirt in a world where showers were prohibited. Taut white horrified faces appeared throughout the ballroom as their own mortality and that of their loved ones registered on each person in the room.

"Now here at home, the crises have escalated. We're going to be releasing specific news coverage to your residences so that you can get caught up and remain current going forward. In some areas, water has been rationed through shutoffs. In other areas we're down to rationed bottled water. Water thefts have resulted in skirmishes among the factions which could easily lead to war.

"With waterflow obstructed by the algae, power production has diminished. Accordingly, we're also rationing that. Once homes or offices reach their daily allocations, power is shut off. As a result, people everywhere are beginning to riot in the streets. "Minister Kolbeck and I are here to answer your questions. Please feel free.

"Olivia Olson, Minister. Programming and computer systems. Will our water and power be rationed for our work?"

"At present, the plan is that this whole Government Complex – the offices and residences – will remain fully operational. Accordingly, you may find significant population increases within these walls with which you'll be forced to deal. The increased traffic may make elevator travel slow, for example. The cafeteria and restaurants may not be able to accommodate you and perhaps sell out sooner. Security forces and procedures will be considerably increased.

"Mikael Matsen, Minister. Microbiologist and worldscaper," he said with aplomb. "I understand that Earth had the ability to terraform as early as the 1960s. Was Annutia terraformed by people on Earth? And could they do it again to eliminate the algae? Does someone still have the connections?"

"Very intelligent questions, sir. You are implying an interesting solution if time wasn't a factor. Old folklore suggests that Annutia's original terraforming took much longer than this xenoforming has taken to have impact.

"I suspect the model for Annutia's terraforming might have come from Earth. However, we can't know whether Earth people organized Annutia's terraforming or Annutian ancestors came from another planet to learn about Earth's capabilities for terraforming and then brought what they learned to Annutia.

I can investigate any connections with Earth that remain to see if there is any means to facilitate what you are proposing. Annalise, could you please take note for me?" Annalise nodded and pulled out her tablet.

"Jordaan Jostad, Minister. Astrophysicist. Also, in the off-world colonization project. How much time do we have left before water and power disappear completely?"

"Jordaan, good to meet you. I know your father. Jostad Sr. and I were talking just last week. Your father tells me you're a gifted inventor of scientific equipment. I'm pleased you've agreed to help us. To answer your question, I estimate the very end would be a year from now at most. However, the degradation in water and power is already very noticeable. You can see from the video that its impact is increasing daily."

"Sven Steensen, Minister Dahl and Minister Kolbeck. Mechanical engineer from power plants with degrees in defense engineering. Are we prepared to mount a war with these invaders if we were to develop the necessary weapons?"

Minister Kolbeck responded with curt military precision. "Yes, sir." The room went silent for a moment in contemplation of this unprecedented possibility.

Sven continued, "What are the plans for military action, Defense Minister Kolbeck, now that the reconnaissance mission is complete?"

"We're currently reviewing our defensive and offensive resources and strategies to determine next actions as soon as possible," Kolbeck answered in his usual brusque manner.

"Do the Miasmians have any form of space or air travel other than the wormhole?" Sven's probe continued.

"None were seen," responded Kolbeck.

"Dania Lind, astrobiologist and terraformer, off-world colonization project. "Did the reconnaissance team encounter any other planets suitable for terraforming or this form of xenoforming during their search?"

"All other celestial bodies examined along the wormhole would require work for the Miasmian population or our own. However, less work than would be required to recover the invaders' planet from their carbon dioxide damage.

"They could use para-xenoforming under a dome on Miasma – if you'll forgive my creation of such a word," suggested Dania.

"But then we'd have to ask the question as to why they didn't do that instead of picking a fight with Annutia," responded Minister Kolbeck. Again, was it an act of war based on survival or imperialistic expansion? Were they just too late to react? Maybe they're happy with their planet the way it is and the remains of other buildings and past waterways were from some previous population. Is the Metropolis in which they live a form of para-xenoforming already? These are the puzzles that we're currently trying to figure out."

"Would it be worthwhile," Mikael queried, "to offer to build them a dome with the water for the algae they have put on Annutia?"

"Do you feel you could do that within the necessary time frame?" Axl questioned. "How could we communicate that to them?"

The potential terraformers within the Breakthru Mission creatives tended to congregate as a group for synergy purposes among the multiple disciplines involved. Accordingly, they were sitting as a group at four tables in the ballroom today. They spoke among themselves for a moment. Mikael stood up again as their usual spokesman and said they felt they could.

"I'll explore that with my people," Minister Dahl responded. He nodded to Annalise to add that to the list.

"Minister Dahl, I'm Marta Kaase. Mechanical engineer for power plants. I'll be working on the power-related aspects of the terraforming solutions. Have Annutians ever sought any off-world colonization other than, as I assume from your previous comments, with Earth?"

"Not to my knowledge, Marta. Annalise, could you please add this to my list for investigation?" Annalise began typing into her tablet.

Henerik Halderson stood up. "What about Earth? Could we migrate there?"

"Earth is already very overcrowded except in places of extreme cold. What kind of life could we have in such cold? In addition, people on Earth have already set in motion some processes which may eventually make Earth uninhabitable. Though certainly not in our generation," he added as an afterthought.

"Once we solve our xenoforming crises, it's more likely that people from Earth would rather start over fresh on Annutia and not make the same mistakes. That could give us some leverage, Henerik," Axl suggested in contemplation. He nodded again at Annalise.

Kellin stood up and asked, "Minister Dahl, if we're working on water filtration, can we arrange access to plants in any of the factions or are we restricted? And if we solve the water issue in some other way, would we sell it to each faction directly or is there some sort of planetary water commission at this point?"

"I like the optimism of your questions, Kellin. You should assume access to any water or power plants. We will make certain that you'll have what you need when you need it."

"Thank you, Minister."

"If you invent water or power solutions, you can come through anyone at Dahl Enterprises. They will know how to get hold of me. I can then take whatever is necessary to the Planetary Council where all factions are represented.

"We'll miss you in the halls of the Government Complex, Kellin. You've become somewhat of a legend. You'll be difficult to replace."

"Thank you, Minister," Kellin said deferentially as is his manner.

Many of the creatives seemed surprised that they had overlooked the strengths of this humble older man. They had initially wondered at Connor's choice to include in the group, uneducated KahlDahr – a janitor so they'd heard and his son, a 20-year-old biology student.

Oh, and a third KahlDahr – Olivia Olson – a lowly programmer with little formal education. The three continually sat together – all with their primitive protruding brow ridges. Apparently, Kellin had lost his wife to illness some years ago. Olivia visited daily to add a needed woman's touch to the residence of the two men.

"Sibylla Lund, Minister Dahl, an electrical engineer who used to work for the Annutian Power Commission."

"Ah, Sibylla. I know your name through my wife Freya. Good to meet you."

"A pleasure, Minister."

"What is your question, Sibylla?"

"What percentage of power is still coming from water power and what percentage is coming from each of the other power sources?"

"We have returned to fossil fuels for 100% of our power even while discovering that this could lead us to the same runaway greenhouse demise as on Miasma. We've reopened all of the old power plants for this purpose."

"Do we have enough fossil fuels remaining?" continued Sibylla. "How long until we run out?"

"Yes, that's the other part of the problem, isn't it?" replied Axl. I think we'll be okay for a few months with supplies on hand. Mining has been restarted, so we may be in luck for a longer period."

"Thank you, Minster," said Sibylla as she sat down. She was visibly discouraged. She knew the consequences for Annutia of the carbon dioxide emissions from burning fossil fuels. Connor knew she'd been part of the committee which determined that the planet must switch over to water power plants ten years ago and eliminate the burning of fossil fuels.

He had thought her connections and experience would be valuable.

Sibylla looked over at Kellin, who was the closest person on the power shortage front that she had as a partner and colleague. They'd been trying to link their solutions for both the water and water power shortages. Her face gradually became more optimistic as Kellin gave her a comforting smile. Connor watched this partnership with interest. He recognized the look on Kellin's face. His friend had figured out some sort of solution. Sibylla recognized it too and was relieved.

Axl looked nervously at his watch. "I'm afraid Minister Kolbeck and I have some urgent matters to which to attend. "However, there is something important I need to say. I want to put an end to our caste system. Allegiance to a race, to a caste, to a class, to a faction has destroyed the lives of too many Annutians. It tears at my heart every time I see examples of the curtailing of the human spirit; of human potential; of human talent. It must end. The waste. The pain. *It has to end.*

"Commander Kane's promotion of talent maximization and the full creative expression of the world's human resources won't just solve our crises, but it will change our society for the better. He has already made this self-actualization a human right on Earth. Everyone there is now much freer to be all they can be. This is a human right I want for every Annutian.

"I want a world in which we build each other up. A world in which we embrace our diversity as the source of our civilization's strength. A world in which each one of us finds the beauty in our differences instead of the fear. A world free of tyranny. A world in which race, religion, physical appearance, sex, education, money, and even nationalism no longer divide us or hold us back.

"I want global unity. In fact, I want more than this. I want global synergy. I want a whole which is greater than the sum of its parts. I want a world in which we rejoice in our common humanity. Our common values. Our common decency. Out of the many, one.

"Look around this room. Other than at the Planetary Council, I've never seen every caste join together as equals to address the needs of the totality. You are the beginning. You must succeed. You must not only save existing life. You must launch a new way of life. Please succeed." Axl's earnestness had pierced the room. There was an uproarious standing ovation by the 144 creatives with Axl's call for success.

"We welcome your questions at any time. We all want to help in any way possible. Thank you,

Commander Kane for allowing us this time," Axl said with a nod as he turned to leave with his team.

"It is we who must thank you, Minister Dahl," responded Connor graciously. "Thank you both for informing and energizing our missions.

"There you have it" said Connor as the Ministers cleared the ballroom. You all have important work to do. Let's get back to your projects. If there are tables which need assistance from Lenore, Daniel, Annalise, or me, please raise your hands."

16

THE WORMHOLE ESCAPE

Lenore put the leftovers from dinner onto a plate as she always did for whomever was on guard that night. It was an infraction of the rules that had become a daily event. She poured a thermos of hot coffee and added two servings of some kind of fruit crisp. Daniel opened the door for her and Jon stood up from the guard table.

"How are you, Jon?"

"Very well, Mrs. Kane. Thank you."

"We had some dinner leftovers to tie you over for the night.

"Wonderful," exclaimed Jon. They will not go to waste."

"Good night, Jon."

"Good night, Mrs. Kane, and thank you."

Daniel closed the door behind her.

Connor emerged from the bedroom in dark clothes. Lenore quickly donned a black jacket so that she too could hide in the night as they travelled to the wormhole.

"What have we got for our light-colored hair?" asked Connor.

Lenore put on a scarf and pulled up the hood of her jacket. Daniel emerged from his suite wearing a black hoodie.

"Good idea," said Connor.

He went back to the bedroom to grab his own hoodie from his workout clothes and put it on.

"Ready?" asked Lenore.

"Ready," both men responded.

Daniel used a kitchen knife to unscrew the cover of the vent providing air-conditioning to this suite and the empty suite next door. Connor clasped his hands together to boost Lenore up through the vent. As she slithered into the vent, she pushed off from Connor's shoulders. In a minute she was gone. Connor and Daniel waited impatiently by the door joining both suites.

Finally, it opened and they passed through to the empty suite. Connor carefully opened the front door and peeked his head out. Because of the turns in the corridor, he could not see Jon outside their suite. However, Connor could see the door to the stairwell almost exactly across from the suite just as Lenore had described.

Connor nodded to the others and started through the door. Daniel held the door as Lenore went next. Connor was holding the stairwell door for her. When she was safely inside, Daniel followed them into the stairwell after quietly closing the suite door behind him.

They all had on sneakers so there was not a sound as they tiptoed down the stairs for a few floors. When they found a floor that was empty, they left the stairwell and went to the freight elevator at the back of the building. Within minutes they were out on the loading dock.

They took back alleys to walk in parallel with Government Avenue. When they hit King Street, they made a right until they found Main Street where the wormhole station was located. They made a left and headed to the wormhole. No one had talked. The streets were deserted. It looked as if they were going to succeed with their escape from the planet.

As they had hoped, the wormhole station was shut down for the night and there seemed to be no security. It would have been easy for the invaders to have gained access to the planet through the wormhole to launch xenoforming assessed Connor.

The three split up and began circling the building to find a way in. Connor and Lenore were together.

"Here," called Lenore. "Boost me up," ordered Lenore. Supporting herself against the wall of the station, she climbed onto Connor's shoulders. She was just high enough to enter through a glass display window. She took a rock from her pocket.

"Cover your eyes, Connor. I'm going to break the glass."

Connor looked down while shards of glass showered all around him. Then he felt Lenore's weight leave his shoulders and she was gone. He shook the glass from his clothes and went around to the main entrance. Daniel was already there having turned the corner just in time to see Lenore enter the station building.

In a minute, the front door opened and they were all three inside. "So, tell us what you know, Lenore," requested Connor.

"The wormhole to Earth is this one on the left. I switch it on here," she said as she flicked various switches on a command console. The left wormhole lighted up. Connor and Lenore looked at each other with big grins. There were ten *bubbles* lined up for passengers. They headed to the furthest one since it was closest to the wormhole.

Before they got in, Daniel called out. "Ah, there's a problem." They came to him. He was reading an instruction manual on the wall. "Here is a list of 12 dates in which the earth wormhole will operate. Apparently, this is not a stable structure. It depends on the orbits of various planets and space bodies. The next date is not for 4 months."

"It turned on fine," said Lenore. "Maybe we should just try it."

"Remember when we stopped three times on the trip here and the lights went off and it was completely silent and still?" reminded Connor. "Then we went off in a different direction? Maybe that's where the orbits of different planets must be lined up. If they're not, maybe we have to sit there for the 4 months until they do line up."

"Or worse," declared Daniel. "We line up with a planet with no oxygen or food."

They looked at each other crestfallen with disappointment. No one spoke for at least a minute. Connor was realizing that the anxious feeling of his resonance that he'd felt earlier was indeed a message not to proceed with their escape plan.

"Now what do we do," asked Daniel.

"Let's go back. No one need be the wiser," said Connor.

"The door of the vacant suite locked behind me," said Daniel in despair.

"Not to worry," said Lenore with a grin. From her jacket pocket she fished a room key card. "I grabbed this from the counter before I opened the adjoining suite door." Connor hugged Lenore. They turned off the wormhole and the station lights and went back out through the main entrance.

Their sleep that night was fretful and full of trepidation. They were prisoners once more on a dying planet. But now they were without the uplifting hope of escape.

17

THE SAVANTING CIRCLES

The creatives filed into the ballroom from their private workrooms for their bi-weekly savanting circles. It's here that they break into groups to help each other to read recent bioflow events to determine their best strategies going forward. They figure out the messages and feedback from the bioflow so they can accelerate their breakthroughs. Reading the bioflow for the projects of others in their circle provides good practice for understanding how the bioflow operates and how to capitalize on it for one's own projects and goals.

Connor spoke to many of the entering creatives before returning to the front of the ballroom with a perplexed look on his face. "Before you begin the updates in your support circles, could I have a show of hands, please.

I'm going to ask you to choose one of these two possibilities – either you've been swimming upstream against the bioflow and been obstructed by block after block to your progress. Or you have been complying with orchestration by the bioflow and you have experienced clusters of coincidences and breakthroughs catapulting your project along.

"No abstainers please. Raise your hand if you have been fighting upstream." Connor turned to Lenore and Daniel with a questioning look. "I know that 30% of you have not ignored our teachings to fight against the bioflow. So, what could be at play here? Does anyone have a hypothesis? No one responded.

"Because time is short let me be more forcefully proactive. Often when novices are working under pressure in crisis situations, they revert back to linear progression rather than savanting's nonlinear approach of serial breakthroughs. How many feel this might explain your blocks?" Only about 5% put up their hands.

"This leaves about 25% of you. Will you please raise your hands once more so I can make another assessment? You've all demonstrated excellent application of the basics of savanting. Therefore, I'm going to assume that you aren't swimming upstream due to lack of knowledge. Show of hands, how many of those swimming upstream are working on weapons of defense or offence after being enticed by Minister Kolbeck?" Seven put up their hands.

"Have any of the six of you experienced flow events to weapon development? They shook their heads. Of those who have experienced the support of the bioflow on their projects, what'd you do when you experienced the kind of blocks that these six have?"

Kellin said, "I tried other directions and hypotheses until I found the flow again."

"Kellin, did you question that you had the right goal or project?" probed Connor.

"Many times," laughed Kellin rolling his eyes. "However, a quick review of the series of flow events or breakthroughs, coincidences, and emotional highs that got me here has so far always confirmed that I was on the right path."

"Good, Kellin. Perfect, in fact. Alright, without flow events to creating weapons and war, let's switch you seven to non-weapons projects or your own projects addressing one of the crises which you would be enthusiastic to pursue.

"My assessment is that the bioflow is indicating that war is not going to bring about the saving of this planet. Either that or there are faster, easier solutions to which the bioflow has given higher priority. Lenore, Daniel, and I will be by your tables to help you to read the patterns faster to get you caught up with the level of development of the other projects.

"Okay, of the remaining 25% that are blocked, let's find out whether your projects are demonstrating viability. Show of hands, how many of you are working on off-world colonization of some sort?"

Terraforming, para-terraforming, launching space stations, and such. Whoa. A lot of you. All of you?" Audience members nodded 'Yes.'

"I think the bioflow has spoken. Off-world colonization is not supported. Of those working on off-world colonization, have any of you had breakthroughs and flow events which suggest the bioflow is supporting some aspect of your work? Yes? Good. So, let's determine what specifically is being supported. Can you tell me about what is flowing so I can assess the pattern of events or theme?

♦♦♦

"Okay. Thank you everyone for sharing your experiences. I may have enough to surmise from the patterns some new hypotheses to test through the action research Kellin has suggested. Here is my assessment. There have been significant flows and breakthroughs around certain processes useful to terraforming but not in their adaptation to off-world locations. Therefore, tell me what your visceral reaction is, what your resonance is, to my suggesting that you apply those impressive terraforming breakthroughs to reinstating the previous terraformed state of Annutia or to any of several crises on Annutia itself.

"Mikael, you've had breakthroughs in viral-assisted gene-splicing and microbe photosynthesis. Bravo. Good work for a recent graduate of microbiology. Can these breakthroughs be applied here on Annutia? Think laterally. Can the algae be converted or killed through similar action? For those who don't know, microbiology is a branch of biology dedicated to the science of plant life including fungi and algae.

"Dania, as an astrobiologist, I think you both have a flow to work together." Giggles from the audience relating to their romance. Connor smiled as he realized what he'd said. "And, in order to accommodate Dania's skills, Mikael, you tended to think of off-world projects. You adapted to her skills. Let's see if she can still experience serial savantflows by adapting her skills to yours, Mikael, here on Annutia.

"I'm going to propose a new hypothesis for testing against the bioflow. That the elements of your work that were flowing might re-terraform Annutia and eliminate the damage and pollution. Is your visceral reaction positive? Is your resonance positive to this hypothesis?"

"It is," responded Mikael as both he and Dania nodded their heads enthusiastically, relieved to be freed from the onerous pathway they'd been fighting daily. "We'll begin working on it immediately."

"Why don't all of those blocked for off-world colonization make a single savanting circle today. Then you can help each other to take what has flowed in your terraforming work to date and use it to generate new projects on Annutia. Marta, how can your innovations for power apply here, for example? Same with you, Sven. And so on."

Kellin raised his hand. "Yes, Kellin."

"Commander, as alluded previously, our project capitalizes on the algae being present. If the terraformers are going to eradicate the algae, do we need to scrap our project?"

"Very good question, Kellin. Why don't we let that decision be made by the bioflow? Why not let it orchestrate your best direction? You've already shown that you understand hypothesis testing and how to reconnect with the bioflow when detached. Why not continue to go with the flow.

"Since Mikael and Dania's flows and your flows and Rolland's are orchestrated by the same bioflow, it's logical to assume that both sets of flows will be synergistic rather than conflicting. This is a good teaching moment.

"Everyone, please take a minute to expand your perception across multiple people to absorb what I'm telling you about the bioflow. There is only one synergistic and synchronized direction in which natural forces are creatively advancing evolution for the survival of our species.

"*Any task you undertake which is supported by the bioflow will always be moving in the same direction as everyone else's task which is being supported by the bioflow*, said Connor with emphasis. "Unless nature loses all logic for order, the bioflow will orchestrate integration, synergy, symbiosis, and synchronization. The tasks will not be in conflict.

"When Mikael changes his goals to on-world, the bioflow will group him with more appropriate systems in the database – which may include you, Kellin. You were outside of his supportive constellation of systems. He changes direction, then you might belong in his constellation."

"Good enough, sir," agreed Kellin.

Olivia's hand went up. "Commander Kane, how did you know these were the two areas that were not being supported?"

"Thank you for this question, Olivia, because it will give me an opportunity to explain subtleties of the new way of operating. I look for agreement from multiple signals. I expect to see logic in the themes of blocks and flows. There were none supporting weapons or off-world terraforming.

"Does my resonance support the on-world direction or the off-world direction? The former. Can the themes of historical bioflow support and savantflows for Dania's and Mikael's past be supported by the new on-world direction? Yes, they can. And so on.

"In addition to my resonance test, I also apply logic. Annutia needs fast solutions. War and terraforming do not seem like fast solutions. When I laid out all the solutions from the creatives side by side in my mind, these two subjects were faded in my mind's eye. They were not as bright or vivid.

"I experienced no flow events internally either. In fact, my own planning and creativity processes were blocked in these two fields. Consequently, I would have no advice to offer them. When have you seen me without advice on how to proceed?" Connor laughed. "There was no creativity flowing on how to make either solution happen quickly.

"I saw patterns of flow events and creative breakthroughs whenever I thought of the sub-projects of the terraformers but could not envisage the completed off-world colony. Therefore, the subprojects must be right projects that would be supported by the bioflow. Consequently, rather than throwing out the whole terraforming project, you extract what is flowing.

"By the next savant circle session, we should have confirmation of this new direction signaled by flow events. But we've already seen this flow from the enthusiasm or resonance of Mikael and Dania moments ago. A weight has been lifted from them. The ideas I expressed to them for adaptation came to them as flow events for their new direction.

"Your consciousnesses have been expanding since you have been spending your days in savantflow. Try to adjust your modus operandi to multisystem thinking to improve your guesses as to the direction of the bioflow. Think beyond bioflow impact on your system alone. The bioflow will look first at what is right for the universe, then what is right for Annutia, then what is right for various Annutia subsystems in priority order, then what is right for your system, and then what is right for your project consistent with your savantflows or maximization. It will try to balance the needs of all those living systems simultaneously.

"This is why popular materialization disciplines cannot work. They're myopic and childlike or primitive in thinking the massive systems of the universe will adjust to the needs of one person's system. They assume separation and fragmentation – that something separate from you can be attracted to you.

"Rather, we must integrate into nature's massive systems to conscript them to achieve faster and bigger goals. The trick is to adjust what goals you are trying to materialize to comply with this hierarchical maximization process of the bioflow.

"Okay. Let's get down to work with your hypothesis testing and savanting circle work. Let's see if I'm right or wrong with respect to the terraformers. Lenore, Daniel, Annalise, and I are going to spend time repositioning the terraform and weapons circles. If there are other groups that need us, please come and find us there."

18
THE BENIGN ALGAE

"You have very much the James Bond look in your tuxedo, my love," said Lenore with an approving smile as she tied his black bow tie. He was wearing the tuxedo he wore when arriving on Annutia from his retirement gala.

"Go do your thing," she said as they entered the ballroom filled with important people in formal attire. Connor went to the stage at the front of the room. Lenore, Daniel, and Annalise went to their seats at the guests-of-honor table front and center next to the stage.

"Welcome, everyone, to the celebration of the success of the Breakthru Mission," greeted Connor. "Please take your seats, ladies and gentlemen". When the room had quieted, he continued. "Welcome to our honored guests. Welcome to our 144 creatives. This is a day to celebrate the incredible breakthroughs from you all which have vanquished Annutia's crises.

"We needed fast solutions to water, power, and food shortages and life-threatening illness. We needed to stop the algae plague inflicted on us by the xenoforming of invaders from planet Miasma. We needed to reverse its damage.

"The rationing is over. Annutians are back in their homes with power and clean water to spare for today and the distant future. Our hospitals are gradually releasing the afflicted. The dead bodies of humans and animals are buried. Our crops and cattle are growing once more. Food sustainability is on the horizon.

"Tonight, all twelve Ministers of the Annutia Planetary Council want to thank the creatives with this celebration of your accomplishments. I've been politely asked by my students to vacate my hosting responsibilities. They've chosen to orchestrate the events of this evening themselves.

"I will therefore abdicate and retire to the background. Marta Kaase will speak first. Marta?" invited Connor as he walked from the stage to take a seat between Lenore and Daniel at his table.

"Thank you, Commander Kane," Marta said as she attached her microphone. "We were taught how to harness the evolutionary flow of all living systems to access a new level of human potential. We were taught how to maximize ourselves in savantflows, so we can merge with nature's maximizing machinery, the bioflow.

The bioflow continuously reorganized or reordered us with the most relevant systems and information. We thus had the information fuel necessary to be combined to generate novel systems.

"Serial breakthroughs, epiphanies, flashes of genius, and creative inspirations suddenly became routine occurrences for us. Life became a magical, miraculous milieu in which euphoria and elation were our normal state of being despite the crises which we were to address.

"We were all amazed at how 144 strangers could so quickly re-combine to create a single engine – a single team – that generated integrated solutions to all the challenges to Annutia's survival. However, this makes sense since Commander Kane, Lenore, Daniel, and Annalise harnessed the bioflow to select each of us for synergy.

"It was incredibly transformative to be part of this Breakthru Mission. It was life-changing. It has created bonds among us that will never be duplicated. And never be broken. What seemed like science fiction was actually a glimpse into true human potential. Our own true potential.

"We watched in microcosm what was possible for the integration of the castes and races of a species when partnered with a bioflow pulling them forward in synergy, synchronization, and symbiosis.

"All man-made fragmentation, persecution, discrimination, and conflict ceased to exist. Unity, synergy, and creative collaboration replaced them. It was an unprecedented experience of unity and community for each and every one of us.

"A lot of our breakthroughs happened simultaneously unbeknownst to the others. Then sitting over lunch or walking back to the residence, the conversations showed how everything coincidentally could be linked together.

"There were almost no extraneous events. Everything folded back into a single integrated solution as if it had been a preconceived project plan. But we never knew the end until we were at the end.

"Yet, amazingly we made very few missteps from what would have been a perfect project plan if we'd been able to make one first. We just stayed in the present and actioned the internal and external indicators moment by moment as we were taught. Today you will hear where we all ended up.

"We have more water and power capacity than before the algae plague. The water shortage is over. We've reclaimed clean water from the mountain, the rivers, the oceans and even from wastewater from our factories and sewers.

"The story is the same for the power shortage. Our previous hydropower plants are back in operation. Plus, we have new power from the rush of mountain water and wastewater. We even have a way to continue to generate power from the cheaper fossil fuels so that they no longer damage our environment or cause the planet to heat up due to greenhouse gases escaping into the atmosphere. We've also added geothermal power, high-altitude wind power, and biofuels that can power our existing gas and oil engines.

"We have many new millionaires in our group and others on their way to millions. Everyone contributed. Everyone experienced a thrilling transformation. Everyone achieved beyond anything we thought ourselves capable.

"We want to thank our esteemed teachers for making this life-changing transformation possible for us. To Lenore, Daniel, and Annalise," said Marta with her glass raised. Audience comments reinforced her appreciation as they also raised their glasses towards the Kane table.

"And finally, to Commander Kane, our brilliant teacher, our enlightened mentor, our catalyst for greatness, our inspirational cheerleader, our fond friend, and our beloved family member.

"Thank you is not enough. You have our eternal gratitude for releasing us to a level of potential, impact, meaning, and reward beyond what we thought was in our future. Your generosity of spirit will never be forgotten. To Connor," Marta said as she raised her glass and smiled at Connor. He raised his glass back at her with a smile and nod.

"I'm now going to call upon two of our most profound world changers to get us started on celebrating what we've developed. I'd like to turn over the stage to Mikael Matsen and Dania Lind, microbiologist and an astrobiologist, respectively, so they may overview their victorious fight against Annutia's enemy, toxic algae."

Algae Detoxification and Mutation – Mikael Matsen *and* Dania Lind, BioVari Inc. was the title that came onto the massive screen stretching across the front wall of the ballroom. Mikael and Dania came to the stage as the audience clapped enthusiastically. Mikael took the microphone as usual and Dania took the remote clicker for the slide show behind them.

Mikael began, "We had been fighting struggle after struggle for weeks. Then Commander Kane read the bioflow patterns of support and block events for our project. He alerted us to the evidence that the terraforming and off-world colonization projects we were pursuing were not being supported by the bioflow for any of the creatives. He suggested that all the potential terraformers get together to determine what had been flowing for us and adapt any breakthroughs we had had for use on-planet rather than off.

"He told us that when we got it right, it would be obvious when the bioflow was supporting us. There would be information, facilitating events, coincidences, and compelling emotional highs. That indeed turned out to be the case. In spades. As soon as we switched goals, there was an avalanche of breakthroughs and epiphanies. It was a roller coaster ride for our team to keep up. We were suddenly being pulled forward faster than we had ever experienced. It was exhilarating. Unprecedented. Unexpected.

"Dania and I had received bioflow support in a process to genetically engineer viruses to transform the DNA of plants and animals for our terraforming project. Could we adapt our methods to transform the toxic algae? Could we develop techniques to inject genetically engineered viruses into the algae DNA to transform them for a variety of purposes?

These were big questions for a planet on which algae were unknown until the xenoforming. "The answers were 'Yes'. We were successful. We were able to convert the invader algae from emitting toxic gases and neurotoxins into benign algae which could benefit our planet and people.

"We had devised the means to inject an engineered virus into the killer algae DNA to mutate and transform their expression from deadly to desirable. With our work, the field of algal virology was born on Annutia."

Vigorous clapping erupted from the audience. This tribute seemed to fluster Mikael who had to search for the best way to continue. "Dania and I founded a company called BioVari Inc. for continuing this work. We've grown quickly into a team of 30.

"Minister Dahl kindly arranged for us to visit the government labs where the algae genome was being analyzed with the hopes of killing them. To date they had been unsuccessful.

"However, I'd noticed something interesting in the genome breakdown work they'd done. A genome, by the way, is the complete set of genes or genetic material or blueprint instructions present in a cell or organism.

"It was apparent that the algae had, at some point in their past, been oxygen producing. Someone or something had turned off those genes. However, it occurred to us that we could genetically engineer an algal virus to turn them back on. This would simultaneously shut off those genes responsible for the emission of the toxins or, more specifically, the neurotoxins that were killing people and animals.

"We used a helicopter to quickly dust algae blooms everywhere with our breakthrough virus transport system. It was at this point that we happened to meet up with Kellin and Rolland over lunch in the dining room. We couldn't help but to share with them our excitement at creating benign algae. It was the Berghs who turned them into proactively beneficial algae.

"Kellin had strong resonance that he had to see the top of Mount Annutia. As soon as he heard about our helicopter work, he begged to come along. Dania and I rolled our eyes because we were continuously being thwarted in having alone time with everyone always being around." Laughter.

"But who can say "No" to Kellin." More laughter. "It ended up being fortuitous for many creatives and the planet that we brought him along.

"Kellin Bergh loves to work with big machinery and systems. Rolland Bergh, his son, is a budding biologist. They share ownership of Bergh Renewable Resources. Let's hear from them next how they caused the BioVari story to continue."

Loud clapping and a standing ovation recognized the phenomenal work of Mikael, Dania, and their team. No one's smile was wider or prouder than that of Connor Kane.

The slideshow title on the large screen now read, *Kellin* and *Rolland Bergh – Bergh Renewable Resources*. Rolland was frightfully nervous. His speech was full of uhs, ahs, and hesitations. However, this young man deserved credit for the breakthroughs he'd achieved. He had therefore succumbed to the pressure of fellow creatives to take the stage.

"We had been concerned that BioVari intended to kill the algae because we'd been supported by the bioflow to capitalize on the blooms. However, Commander Kane had explained that the bioflow would not support two mutually exclusive directions. Therefore, we should allow the bioflow to redirect us from conflict to synergy. That's exactly what happened.

"Before our lunch with Mikael and Dania to celebrate their viral DNA delivery system, we had already been working on ways to interconnect algae power and water purification plants.

"After the lunch, the first thing we did was to populate a number of algae farms with BioVari's benign algae. We located them next to the fossil fuel power plants which Annutia has to use in place of hydropower because of algae blocking the waterflow of the Kalix River.

"We wanted to syphon off the CO2 emissions from burning fossil fuels. Rather than letting them cause a greenhouse effect that would warm the planet, we wanted to use them for positive applications.

The screen changed to *Algae Biofuels* – Bergh Renewable Resources.

"The CO2 from burning fossil fuels is a nutrient that feeds the benign algae. They convert it to oxygen. We were keen to harness that process to create biofuels which would be cleaner than today's fuels and would be renewable. To produce cleaner energy in the form of biodiesel, methane or ethanol," Rolland added hesitantly as he recalled what he had studied to say.

"I'd already determined that this new xenoforming algae species was 50% oil. I'd created and tested algae fractionation processes for converting this oil into gas, jet fuel, or diesel fuel. It worked perfectly as fuel for cars, diesels, boats, and indeed all machinery requiring gas or oil. No modification to today's engines was required.

"The algae, or more correctly, microalgae, are very small aquatic organisms that convert sunlight into energy. The microalgae store energy in the form of natural oils. By adjusting their environment, they can be stimulated to increase their oil production for conversion into biofuels. The result is an alternative, renewable energy source consistent with our brand for Bergh Renewable Resources.

"I just needed help to develop the means to make this fuel production economically viable. That's where BioVari came in again. We asked them to engineer genetic modifications to their new benign algae for improved biofuel production. Obviously, if we succeeded, it was going to be quite lucrative. It would be like owning your own oil and gas wells and refineries. Who knew that a biologist could become an oil tycoon?

"My dad and Jordaan Jostad generated several breakthroughs in the design of the plant systems for producing the biofuels. We're now building our patented algae-based biorefineries to capture the flue gases from several different industrial facilities as our raw materials.

"We are pleased that we're able to use algae to lock away the greenhouse gases that have been destroying our planet. I will let my dad, Kellin Bergh, continue the story of Bergh Renewable Resources and our lucrative partnership with BioVari Inc."

More clapping for Rolland's work.

As Kellin came to the stage, the screen title changed to *Clean Water from Wastewater and Seawater* – Bergh Renewable Resources.

"Thank you, Rolland. The Bergh algae farms could almost completely sequester the CO_2 emissions from the burning of fossil fuels to slow greenhouse gas emissions. This was only our company's first improvement to the environment. The second was through the production of cleaner burning biofuels.

"The third benefit of our algae farms was that BioVari's benign algae could also purify wastewater. Wastewater hinders the growth of most kinds of plants. However, it provides the nutrients that help to grow the new algae species.

"Algae photosynthesis fueled by those nutrients actually cleans the wastewater so efficiently that it can be used for drinking water. Reclaimed wastewater can become a new source of water to address the planet's water shortage. And it can be provided on a city by city basis from the sewage each generates. It is a renewable resource.

"To get the government contracts for wastewater purification to drinking water, we did an experiment for them. We sealed raw sewage water in large plastic bags with some of BioVari's reengineered algae in them. We then floated these bags in a polluted pond and let the sun cause photosynthesis in the algae.

"One week later, the sealed bags were opened for testing by Annutia Waterworks. The water inside was purer than even that coming out of their own water filtration plants. Since we were there, we also added the benign algae to the pond and have since eliminated its pollution."

The screen title shifted to something unexpected: *Food from Algae* – Bergh Renewable Resources.

"The fourth benefit of our algae farms will surprise you given where we started with the deadly algae. Bergh Renewable Resources is also using a segment of our algae farms for high-grade certified organic high-protein algae for people food – snacks, soups, salads, noodles, drinks, and more. We are also producing pill supplements.

"The nutrient-dense algae have the potential for eliminating the planet's food shortages with lower costs and greater nutrition. During the crises, the absence of water eliminated crops and animals. Algae neurotoxins also killed many animals. Once we marketed to overcome the public's fear of algae, there was an immediate receptivity to purchase algae feed for cattle. As we made it tastier, the people market emerged looking for this cheap, plentiful, nutritious food.

"One gram of algae – about the equivalent in a tiny tablet – contains the nutritional equivalent of 1,000 grams of fruits and vegetables. Minister Dahl was instrumental in our securing large government orders to provide algae food to the breadlines. This has helped to lock algae food into the marketplace. Thank you once more, Minister Dahl for helping us in this and so many ways."

The slide on the screen changed to *Minerals from Wastewater and Seawater* – Bergh Renewable Resources *and* Henerik Halderson Biochemists

"Bergh Renewable Resources had both seawater and wastewater running through our plants to feed the algae. Both types of water are complex cocktails of valuable minerals that can be mined for profit. We therefore partnered with Henerik Halderson and his team of chemists to help us to extract them. They had invented a finer water filtration system that was powerful enough to remove even the deadly algae neurotoxins and pathogens.

"First, we asked them to adapt their metal-organic framework (MOF) membranes to remove salt from seawater so we could quickly create another source of fresh water for a thirsty planet. Then we asked them to change the specificity of their membranes to extract the valuable minerals.

"Lithium, for example, is in high demand for the lithium-ion batteries that power everything from smartphones to electric cars. Lithium ions are abundant in seawater and wastewater. Henerik's process therefore competes well with a mining industry which currently uses inefficient chemical treatments to extract lithium from rocks and brines.

"Henerik had been a biochemistry dropout when he was recruited to the Breakthru Mission. He has since received an honorary degree for his revolutionary innovations with metal-organic frameworks (MOFs), a next-generation material with the largest internal surface area of any known substance. MOF membranes can mimic the filtering function or 'ion selectivity' of organic cell membranes.

"Henerik, could you please stand up, so we may thank you for your world-changing inventions. We are all so proud of this young man." Applause were fast and furious for Henerik. No one had even conceived of Henerik's filtration solutions to the water crisis.

"We'll now take a brief nature break before continuing with the major breakthroughs that have addressed the power shortage. A buffet and cocktails will follow in the Library for the creatives and Ministers. While on break, I invite you to view all the awards won by the creatives over the last few months that are on display around this room."

Connor watched with pride as many guests gravitated to the easels holding the glassed-in frames of the awards won by his creatives. There were even some cancelled checks worth millions of dollars and contracts to generate more millions, each in their own glass frames.

Part of him was happier than he'd ever been. Unfortunately, there was a part of him that was filled with foreboding. It was not from any information of which he'd become aware. Rather, he'd had a series of innocuous blocks over the last few days surrounding the evening's Library celebration for which he had no explanation as yet.

19
POWER AND WATER

When everyone returned from the break, a new title appeared on the screen behind Kellin: *The Sewer Power-and-Water Pipelines* – Bergh Renewable Resources *and* Stinar Solar. When the room quieted, Kellin continued.

"Before the break, we started to reveal our new sources of clean water from wastewater and seawater to address the water shortage. We harnessed these same water solutions to simultaneously address the power shortage.

"When Bergh Renewable Resources won the contracts from various cities for purifying their wastewater, we began researching local sources for the wastewater and locations nearby for our algae farms where we could purify it. It suddenly dawned on me that I was often looking at rushing water in every sewage system.

"I realized that if we installed turbines and pumps within the pipes to speed the water even more, we could generate local hydropower." The fan-like turbines appeared on the screen behind Kellin. "From the slide you can see that water flows through a turbine, spins it, which in turn activates a generator to produce electricity."

"Greg and his company, Stinar Solar, were happy to assist with his famous solar-powered turbines. For negligible costs, these could accelerate the flow of wastewater through the sewer pipes to make it a source of hydropower.

"At the same time Greg and I were figuring out this wastewater source of drinking water and power, the helicopter trip with Mikael and Dania coincidentally reinforced and strengthened what we were planning.

"As Commander Kane forewarned, the bioflow organizes relevant information systems in the same direction for synergy. It tends not to harbor systems in conflict."

The screen title revealed the coincidences to which Kellin was referring: *The Mountain Power-and-Water Pipeline* – Bergh Renewable Resources *and* Henerik Halderson Biochemists *and* Stinar Solar.

"It was indeed serendipitous when Dania and Mikael included me in their momentous helicopter trip. First it was an honor to be part of the event that changed the future of our planet and indeed all

Annutians. They dusted the deadly algae with BioVari's genetically engineered virus in order to detoxify the species.

"From the helicopter, we discovered that the algae blooms ended before the source of the Kalix River high on Mount Annutia. It must have been too cold for them to live up there. We suddenly realized that we may have located the only place on the planet where there was algae-free water.

"When we flew over the peak of Mount Annutia, I could see three water towers or reservoirs circling the mountain midway down from the top. I wondered if I could pipe the algae-free water from above the toxic algae line down to those three reservoirs.

"First, I thought 'No' since it'd take a lot of time to dig into the ground to lay enough pipe. We'd also need to buy or lease land rights from all the property owners to take a direct route to the reservoirs. This would take even more time and the costs would be prohibitive.

"Then, as we flew home down the Kalix River, I saw the solution. We could suspend the new lightweight polymer pipes along the right-of-way for the hydro power lines down to these three water reservoirs. An aerial piping infrastructure could be quickly and easily installed. It could also be quickly dismantled when the water shortage was over.

"Elevation could prevent the vandalism which had arisen around the world as people were driven by extreme thirst to steal water. From the reservoirs, the fresh water could feed into the water pipeline networks already attached to them.

"The Planetary Council agreed in principle to allow us to pursue this solution. However, they required strict water purification and treatment standards for water entering the reservoirs. We went away and did some more thinking. We then made our pitch again with a little help from some fellow creatives.

"Gregor Stinar was one of the original terraformers which the bioflow supported for his inventions just as it had with Mikael and Dania. This support was despite the blocks to the off-world terraforming projects. Greg had just graduated with a Masters in bioscience engineering and hadn't yet found employment when Commander Kane snatched him up. He specializes in environmental technology.

"One of Greg's inventions at Stinar Solar which the bioflow supported with breakthroughs and information coincidence collisions was the development of a revolutionary water purification system – a solar disinfection method. It uses the sun to catalyze a chemical process which kills 100% of the bacteria in the water in just 15 minutes. Exposing titanium dioxide, zinc oxide, and silver nitrate to ultraviolet radiation from the sun generates a photocatalytic composite that cleans water."

Kellin continued. "To Greg's amazing solar inventions, we added Henerik Halderson's incredible metal-organic frameworks (MOF) membranes. Water filtration through these membranes could be so fine that even the deadly algae neurotoxins and pathogens could be removed. We were able to demonstrate to the Planetary Council that this clean water piped from above the toxic algae line on the Kalix River was going to be purer than any other source on the planet.

"To this improved water treatment pitch, we added yet another perk. Power. When we were brainstorming the revised pitch to the Council, we realized gravity would be propelling the clean water to rush down the steep mountain pipeline.

"If we accelerated this water flow with solar-powered turbines as we had done in the sewers, we could generate substantial hydropower. Since we were already using the hydro right-of-ways, we could easily connect to the existing generators, equipment, lines, and distribution grid to distribute power.

"We were now able to offer the Planetary Council a mountain power-and-water pipeline running on sunlight, a renewable resource. The pipeline could supply electricity not only for the cities but also for all the remote villages and farms on the way down the mountain which didn't have electricity even before the algae plague. The benefits of inexpensive power and water would civilize new areas and make more territories of the planet habitable and prosperous.

"Take a look at the pictures on the screen. The only technology inside the water pipes would be five-bladed spherical turbines, 42 inches in diameter, made of stainless steel and composite fiber.

"Most of the other parts — the seals, bearings, grid connections, and so on — would sit outside the pipes. Notice that the whole system is designed so that the water delivery is never disrupted. Solar-powered turbines installed inside the water pipes also come with no environmental costs. Compare them with the large footprint and disruption of hydroelectric dams, for example, which kill fish and other wildlife.

"Needless to say, the Council decided to invest millions of dollars into our solution. Then, with the help of a massive number of volunteers, donations of resources, and the release of materials produced for other customers by manufacturers – thank you again Minister Dahl for interceding – the mountain pipeline was actually installed and operational in under four weeks. At least 30% of Annutia's suburban homes had their water and power restored through this initiative." Clapping from the audience.

"Both the aerial and sewer water-and-power solutions could now be offered to cities and towns all over the planet. The planetary benefits from this multidisciplinary partnership of creatives is just beginning."

"Greg, could you please stand and take a bow for your world-changing solar inventions?" Greg accommodated Kellin's request and stood to the roar of applause, "Bravos" and "Congratulations" from the audience. Connor stood to clap inciting an audience-wide ovation.

He stood for Kellin as much as Greg for this ingenious initiative. He suspected that was the feeling of the other audience members as well. Despite Kellin's humble graciousness to Greg, everyone knew that it would not have succeeded or succeeded so quickly without Kellin.

To move the program along, Kellin continued before clapping had stopped. "There are some additional creatives I want to recognize for making possible the implementation and synergy of the various divisions of Bergh Renewable Resources. I have a phenomenal team.

"I think all would agree that Sibylla Lund deserves recognition. Sibylla is an electrical engineer laid off from the hydropower plants when the algae plague prevented the use of hydropower. Sibylla is the first female and first Varunian to become an electrical engineer.

"Sibylla has 20 years of experience in power plants. It was her knowledge of the power plants, equipment, and grid that enabled the rapid integration of our various new power sources from the sewers, the mountain pipeline, and the geothermal plant which you will learn about shortly.

"Olivia Ohlson also deserves mention for the creation, adaptation, installation and integration of all of the computer systems required at all of the Bergh plant installations. This is a massive job executed in weeks not years due to her rare gift for both detail and expansive thinking.

"Until discovered by Commander Kane, Liv was a junior programmer for the government. Given her incredible inventiveness, execution creativity, systems thinking, and span of purview, Liv was obviously a diamond in the rough. A programming prodigy overlooked by the pre-Kane discrimination based on birth rather than talent. We are grateful she was freed to help save the planet. Could you please stand, Olivia? Enthusiastic applause.

Connor was pleased that Kellin's personal and financial success had emboldened him to assume a new position in the global power structure. He was ready to elevate talent and suppress persecution. He would not have spoken about KahlDahr discrimination before the Breakthru Mission.

"I also need to recognize astrophysicist Jordaan Jostad who has flourished in our playground of massive machines and systems underlying the Bergh

Renewable Resources plants. Jordaan is the most gifted machine designer I've ever encountered. Together we were able to quickly adapt existing machinery to the first-ever algae processing plants for algae biofuels, algae food processing, algae water purification, and mineral and salt extraction.

"We also created the first ever geothermal plant in weeks not months. "Together we achieved unprecedented speeds of innovation by jury rigging machines designed for other purposes to fit our needs within short time-frames. Could you please stand, Jordaan, so we may recognize you for your extraordinary achievements and express our gratitude?" Applause.

Kellin went on to praise the work of many other creatives who had contributed to his massive synergy complex. The largest group were the execution creatives which Commander Kane had touted. These are the execution savants who can implement any project in known or unknown territory faster than even experts in the field.

Kellin had shrewdly persuaded anyone in the Mission creatives who had this gift to join his team. They could partner with the bioflow when he wasn't there and take the same decisions that he would take in his absence. What more could a leader ask?

And Kellin was the iconic model of the gifted execution creative. What achievement junkie could resist working at top speed on world-saving projects with Kellin? Together they could implement Kent Bergh projects at almost superhuman speeds – catapulted ahead by clusters of coincidences and quantum leaps.

Connor loved that Kellin now found his work thrilling and was being recognized for that work. There were still all these big machines and systems in his life with which he was addicted to tinkering at the Government Complex. *Except now he owned them.* Kellin was having an encore beyond anything he'd imagined for himself.

Kellin announced a second nature break. Applause resounded for Kellin. He was a force of nature thought Connor. He was not just the force behind his own company, and behind his son's accomplishments, he was the force behind most of the projects in the Breakthru Mission.

Kellin seemed to have unlimited capacity, unlimited creativity, unlimited compassion, unlimited generosity, and unlimited ideas and advice. Ayn Rand's street sweeper protagonist, Equality 7-2521, a.k.a. Prometheus, in *The Anthem* was a heroic world changer. However, he didn't compare with this janitor of Annutia's Government Complex.

Annalise had arranged the seating plan for all of the Ministers and VIPs attending. At the Kane table, Connor was seated between Daniel and Lenore.

Lenore sat to Connor's right beside Axl. Freya was between Axl and Azurite Chief of State Einar Nyhus. Annalise sat between Nyhus and, of course, Daniel, who was beyond happy to spend time with Annalise. Was she interested in both? The tables could accommodate eight people so she could have brought someone . . . .

As he was analyzing the life of his understudy, Connor overhead Nyhus speaking to Annalise. "I knew Kellin only as the janitor, a KahlDahr with a primitive protruding brow.

I thought I was a good judge of talent. It never occurred to me that Kellin was capable of what he has accomplished to save Annutia," confessed Nyhus. "I certainly couldn't have done it and it's closer to my job than his. Was Kellin always able to see the interconnections of such a massive synergistic organization?"

Annalise replied, "He was indeed much more talented than most realized. At the beginning of the Breakthru Mission, he could see the breadth of a large complicated system. He could repair it, but I don't believe he had the creativity to design such systems or conceive of new frontiers for their use.

"Through serial savantflows Kellin's consciousness has expanded to the point where he can hold the entirety of Bergh Renewable Resources in his mind and know how it should be structured to benefit the totality of the planet.

"I've enjoyed having a front row seat to see the incredible transformation of every creative. In comparing the before and after of extending themselves with the machinery evolving all living systems, I find it frightening how little of human potential is being used by most people. We have a wealth of untapped capacity in the population of the planet."

"I see now why Minister Dahl is so keen to duplicate Kane's maximization of Earth's human resources," pondered Nyhus. "Human beings are our greatest renewable resources, aren't they?"

Annalise nodded her agreement. As she caught Connor watching her, they smiled at each other. They were both thrilled to have worked on this mission about which they were both so passionate. This was also their day to celebrate what they had achieved.

20

THE UNEXPECTED POWER

On the return from the nature break, the title slide read *The Geothermal Power Plant – Bergh Renewable Resources*. Kellin was still on the stage to continue.

"From the helicopter at the source of the Kalix River atop Mount Annutia, I noticed that there was steam rising from rocky caverns below into the cold mountain air. I asked the pilot to get me a little closer. Suddenly I realized what I was looking at. I couldn't believe our good fortune.

"I had researched geothermal electricity for heating and powering this Government Complex where we are living and working now. It was too expensive in this location to drill down a couple of miles into the planet's molten core. What I was looking at on Mount Annutia was a cluster of steaming faults, vents, fissures, and hot springs. This meant the planet's core was heating water right at the surface. No drilling would be required.

"Geothermal energy uses the steam from water being heated by the planet's core magma. That steam spins large turbines which are connected to generators. These generate electricity. Connect it to the existing power infrastructure and we are good to go.

"Expenses for generating the electricity from this renewable resource would be minimal. One would simply have to install the turbines and generators to be driven by the steam. The resulting electricity could be channeled into the hydro grid.

"I figured with the world crises I could get the turbines and generators we needed quickly from the front of the production line. This could be a very lucrative geothermal power plant which I suspected I could easily sell to investors. If investors weren't interested, I was confident that I could sell it through a crowd equity website to quickly source the partners or investments I needed.

"Investors were indeed interested. Thank you to those in attendance tonight. As a result of your generosity, all of this came to pass. Now we have the first geothermal plant on the planet.

"We recruited so much help in this crisis to build this geothermal plant and there were so many volunteers that we completed it in seven weeks from conception to power delivery. This is unheard of. Normally it takes months for a plant of this size.

"Right now, the plant is providing good clean power from a renewable source for over 500,000 homes in another 30% of the planet beyond the 30% of the mountain pipeline." Spontaneous applause broke out from the audience even though it was evident that Kellin was not yet finished.

"Our biggest challenge to launching the geothermal plant was the reclusive hillbilly hermit who owned the land. Mr. Billy Bob Blixt." Laughter from the creatives in the know. "Billy Bob had not seen anybody for years. He had no electricity. He had no internet. He had no phone. He heated his home and got his hot water from a nearby hot spring.

"We had to entice Billy Bob on a special trip to stay at our residences here to introduce him to another way of living. We wanted him to see all the technology and appliances he could use if he had electricity.

"We played video games with him; let him watch TV; and took turns getting him hooked on the internet like everybody else. Everybody on the creatives floor pitched in to help cultivate Billy Bob's addiction. It took four days for him to say he wanted everything we had in his home.

"We set up a deal to buy part of his land by providing him with free electricity, internet, phone, running water, and every appliance and electronic gadget that he wanted. He had very little need for money. Fortunately, his understanding of what land and other things were worth were within our budget.

"Billy Bob is now living a completely new life at age 54. He is now a very social guy. He has a lot of friends here now, so he has good reason to have a phone. We've even connected him with family he never knew he had. He eats lunch for free at the cafeteria at the geothermal plant most days and has made lots of friends there.

"We've also provided Billy Bob with the equipment and training he needs to mine the geothermal gold which is scattered throughout his property. Billy Bob Blixt is now a wealthy man loving life and enjoying new purpose. Here's to Billy Bob Blixt for making Annutia's first geothermal plant possible," said Kellin raising his glass. "Here's to another unexpected Breakthru Mission millionaire." Laughter from the audience as they raised their glasses.

Amidst the toast, the title slide on the screen changed to read *Geothermal Mining* – Bergh Renewable Resources (B.R.R.).

"To algae oil mining and the mining of wastewater and seawater, B.R.R. now adds geothermal mining or the mining of hydrothermal ore deposits. Gold was the best legacy of past volcanism on Mount Annutia.

"Minerals and metals such as silica, lithium, manganese, zinc and sulfur, mercury, arsenic, boron, and antimony, magnesium, and more are now being extracted from geothermal fluid to obtain marketable byproducts.

"These geothermal systems acted as a natural distillery in the subsurface. They dissolved trace amounts of gold, silver, and other rare elements from their host rocks. These elements were then deposited at places where changes in temperature, pressure, or composition favored precipitation.

"We now have turbines within sewer pipelines, the mountain pipeline and the geothermal plant. However, this next unprecedented use of turbines will catch you by surprise. Mechanical engineer and CEO of WindPower Inc., Sven Steensen, will reveal all." Applause again for Kellin as he left the stage to return his table with Rolland, Olivia, Sibylla and friends.

The title slide changed on the screen to *Flying Air Turbines* – Sven Steensen, WindPower Inc. as Sven came to the stage.

"Thanks Kellin. Within a few months you've transformed from maintenance engineer to captain of industry. Your success is well deserved. Your story is inspirational, sir. And all the more so because you were instrumental in the success of so many other creatives. Your contribution to the saving of our planet has been massive. Thank you, Kellin Bergh." More applause and a standing ovation. Then Sven continued.

"New innovations in the effectiveness of wind farms are making them a more common sight on Annutia. The wind is used to turn large turbines which then turn a generator to produce electricity. Wind power may seem like an ideal renewable resource to many to solve the power shortage.

"However, Annutia's winds on water and land are weak and inconsistent. They are therefore unreliable as a power source. So, I decided to challenge myself to come up with a better solution. I'm a mechanical engineer. You've seen the slides of what Kellin's turbines look like for his sewer pipes, seawater pipes, and mountain pipes. Each turbine is like an egg-beater within a cylinder." Photos came up on the screen to clarify.

"Kellin had this small turbine sitting in his workroom within the light-weight polymer pipe for the mountain pipeline. This gave me the idea to put these same light eggbeater turbines into inflatable cylinders for wind power. I guess you could say I re-combined existing information systems fed by the bioflow to create this novel information system.

"These new wind turbines can then be flown 1000 to 2000 feet above the planet where the winds are 30 times stronger and 90% more continuous than on the planet's surface. These high-altitude wind turbines could therefore generate much more power than those on land or water.

"And they could be flown anywhere. In remote areas that are too far away from the planetary electrical grid to access power, for example. We could create flying wind farms that could float enough wind turbines to power any towns or villages without taking up any of their real estate.

"You can see from the photo on the screen behind me what Annutia's first high-altitude wind turbine looks like. We call it a *Flying Air Turbine* or F.A.T. It's a circular, 35-foot-long inflatable shell made of heavy-duty fabric. It is inflated with helium which lifts the turbine to high altitudes. It's completely autonomous. It self-adjusts to position for optimal wind speeds. It even self-docks in emergency situations.

"It has a tether that holds it to the ground. The power from the turbine travels down through this tether to the power grid or to some power storage box on the ground. "Now here is the exciting bonus benefit of the Flying Air Turbine. *It provides a platform for internet and phone services even in remote areas where there is currently access to neither,*" Sven exclaimed emphatically. It was obvious to everyone that he was thrilled with what he'd developed.

"These F.A.T.s can be deployed *anywhere* quickly. For disaster relief organizations. For the military bases wherever they are needed. For the oil & gas and mining industries operating in remote locations. For remote villages in developing nations.

"We've all learned so much from Kellin about how to harness the bioflow for rapid-fire installation. Kellin is the ultimate execution creative. So, he knew to snatch up all the execution creatives while the rest of us assumed we could do everything ourselves," Sven said facetiously. Laughter.

"So, it was a bit of a challenge for me to persuade Kellin to lend me some of them to speed the installation of high-altitude wind turbine farms wherever they could do the greatest good.

"Kellin is such an achievement junkie. He's addicted to high-speed action. And now he's made addicts of all of them. Finally, they relented. Some of them agreed to work on my project part-time 'only if they could continue to operate at the same speed.'

"I was thrilled. These phenomenal implementers did such an incredible job that we had over a thousand high-flying turbines installed within the first month. Then their creativity went over the top to implement even more. Something from the heart.

"They came up with one of their most endearing ideas: *The Adopt-a-Power-Balloon* program. It quickly became an overwhelming success that has changed the connectiveness of our planet. The goal is to get electricity, internet and phone service quickly wherever you want it.

"Many people couldn't stay connected with family and friends without these three services. The underprivileged and the developing areas will not raise their economic status without them. So, we set it up that families and benefactors can choose the locations where they want to tether their very own power balloon. We'll then price out the project for the installation and service.

"If you can afford the initial and ongoing services, you will own your own F.A.T. You will get to name it and determine its future. If not, we'll set up a fundraising platform for your F.A.T. on our crowd-sourcing or crowd-equity website. Crowd-sourcing if you want donations so that you can retain ownership. Crowd equity if you want investing partners.

"Once you accumulate enough donations or investments, we'll get it installed as quickly as possible. We'll equip it with internet and phone services to parts of the world that don't have it yet.

"If you haven't been able to communicate with your relatives, friends, or village back home, now you can buy them a power balloon which could allow that to happen sooner rather than later. By selling advertising on the outside of each blimp, it's possible to be self-sufficient in funding your annual maintenance costs.

"So far, investors have adopted over 4000 flying power blimps to date thus spreading power and connectedness across the planet. Global businesses have been launched from primitive villages. Families, friend, and lovers have been reunited. Knowledge has been shared with those who've had no access to it. Solutions have been found that vastly improved quality of life. Those in trouble have been rescued, received what they needed, or gotten medical assistance, for example.

"Please join me in thanking these phenomenal execution creatives. Olof, Niklas, Lennart, Sonja, Tova, and Vita please stand.

Standing ovation. The entire ballroom erupted in cheers and clapping. Many called out accolades. Many had tears in their eyes for this phenomenal opportunity to reach out to their own relatives.

"Families, friends and guests, please stay and enjoy a cocktail party here in the ballroom. Creatives, Ministers and invited Breakthru Mission participants, please join us in the Library for libation, levity, and a buffet dinner."

"What a great finish to a great celebration," Connor sighed to Lenore.

"Between Billy Bob Blixt and the reunion of families," said Lenore. "So heartwarming," said Lenore blinking away her tears of joy. Connor gave her a hug and with his hand on her back began to guide her towards the Library.

Azurite Chief of State Nyhus joined Commander Kane as he was winding his way towards the Library through the groups congregating over cocktails.

"You must have great leadership skill to have bonded different races into such a mutually supportive team in such a short time. It's unprecedented on this planet. It's a challenge for me to bond even the Azurite people. I spend so much of my time resolving conflicts."

"Thank you, Minister. I can lead when necessary, but I don't believe that's how the multi-race creatives have bonded. As a biological anthropologist, I have other levers at my disposal.

"For example, if everyone is being orchestrated in the same direction by the same bioflow evolving humanity, that will bond people. It will remove the divisions. It will create a common culture and shared goals. Conflicts and blocks mean you're going in the wrong direction, so they'll be resolved by compliance with the bioflow.

"I can take the manual approach and give everyone the pitch as to why they want to integrate into the bioflow evolving humanity. I can tell them how much faster they'll achieve goals. I can tell them how they'll operate beyond their potential. I can tell them how it will bond them into a community. I can then tell them how to merge with the bioflow. In the manual approach, I could even try to demand that everyone comply with the bioflow.

"Or I can invoke the automatic approach. When each person is applying their strongest most rewarding talents to the most meaningful work, they will slip into savantflow – a highly gratifying and highly addictive state of peak performance. They will merge automatically with the bioflow.

"That's when it really becomes exhilarating. It's as if reality is helping you. Accelerating you. Providing phenomenal coincidences that catapult you past thousands of steps you thought you had to take. Or catapulting you in the direction of solutions you never even considered.

"Spend some time doing your best work at your fastest speed of achievement and growth in this savantflow-bioflow state and you'll be hooked. Biochemically, emotionally, electromagnetically. You'll be hooked in the same way heroin addicts. As this state becomes your new daily modus operandi, you go through a transformation – one which includes expanded consciousness and changes in your frequency.

"When you've experienced this thrilling transformation, you have a special bond with others who've shared that experience. One lives by a different language, a different protocol, different goals, and different values and beliefs.

"The direction of the bioflow bonds them for sure. But being fully self-actualized in the same way with the same shared beliefs, values, and modus operandi consistent with the way human beings have evolved to operate at their maximum is what unifies them. This is a replacement culture which glorifies talent, contribution, meaning, synergy, synchronization and symbiosis and could care less about race, creed, or any other differences."

"Creating a culture – a system of beliefs, shared goals and meaning is an oft overlooked way of leading," posited Nyhus.

"How very insightful, Minister Nyhus," replied Connor, knowing full well that Einar Nyhus had figured out the secret to his leadership success.

"Back at you, Commander Kane," smiled Nyhus.

21
THE SHATTERED CELEBRATION

The Breakthru Mission creatives and their supporters and benefactors trailed from the white and bright ballroom to the dark oak-paneled Library to continue their celebrations with food and drink and camaraderie. The room was clothed for opulence – a fitting context for deferentially honoring those who had contributed so significantly to saving the planet.

Walls of dark-bound tomes suggesting age and wisdom punctuated the wood panels. The deeply honeycombed indentations of the vaulted ceiling in the same dark oak completed the cocoon-like coziness of the large room. The Library was obviously appointed to provide a sense of history to a planet that was still in its infancy.

Beneath the elaborate and expansive crown molding framing the ceiling, a row of windows bordered the room high above the paneling and shelves of books. If it had been daylight, they would have flooded the room with a very different light. For now, they merely reinforced the darkness of the cocoon.

The old-world elegance of the Library was epitomized by the blazing fire in the floor-to-ceiling black granite fireplace which anchored the room. Its inviting glow danced off the multi-faceted polish and sheen of the room's accoutrements. A colony of crystal chandeliers bejeweled the ceiling to add a glittering luminescence to the firelight.

The Library was dominated by a massive built-in bar structured from carved dark oak panels and topped with a heavy black granite slab to match the fireplace. Brilliant tiny spotlights embedded within the ceiling created the breadth of light that magnetized everyone to congregate there for conversation.

Seating vignettes grouped for peace and privacy had been pushed to the wall around the large Library room to permit the long table of a lavish buffet in the center of the room. Luxuriously deep and tufted leather couches were paired with proud wingback chairs and coffee and side tables of every description.

Lamps darkened by ornate shades highlighted each seating arrangement. The sectionings were also accompanied by a population of other chairs – Bergère, Lawson, tub, and club – offering a potential fit for any bottom and back. Hassocks strewn throughout added to the welcoming warmth of the relaxed elegance.

The buffet table teemed with the most succulent dishes. Each was spotlighted by their own silver-encased lights which shielded the glare from the side and above to minimize detraction from the ambience created by the chandeliers, fireplace, and bar.

As the bulk of the creatives and Council Ministers burst into the room, Connor turned to look at his students with affection and satisfaction. They had each excelled in their challenge to transcend their history to crush the crises facing their world.

More than this, he loved the community they had formed. They were family. Everyone was now congregated in elation chatting about the success of their various undertakings. Camaraderie was everywhere. Connor so enjoyed watching their joviality and pride of achievement. This post-transformation success was his jam.

Axl stepped onto the dais next to the bar where it could share in its ceiling lights. He identified and thanked the many VIPs in attendance for their contributions and support. To close, he thanked Connor from his heart.

An uproar interrupted Connor's discussion with Jostad, Sr. who wanted to purchase the Annutian rights to his book, *Savanting*, which was just about complete.

Out of the corner of his eye, Connor saw that Mikael was on one knee with a ring proffered to Dania. Connor quickly excused himself and Lenore so they could share in their friends' happy event.

Dania responded with a teasing grin, "Now, that I know you'll be able to afford me, Mikael, I accept." No one was surprised. But everyone laughed and clapped and said congratulations in enjoyment of the inevitable moment.

"She said 'Yes'", exclaimed an elated Mikael with his arms raised in triumph. Dania held up the large diamond ring on her left hand with a blushing grin of sheer joy on her face. Kellin and Sibylla joined the group.

"Beat you again, Mikael" joked Kellin when the roar of the group had abated. He held up Sibylla's left hand which also sported a diamond engagement ring. A pleasant shock registered on the faces of both Mikael and Dania and the remaining spectators. No one had seen this coming. A Varunian and a KahlDahr. Was that a first?

"Upstaged by the Berghs even in this," laughed Mikael. "Must be something contagious in our partnership."

Dania gently grasped Sibylla's wrist amiably. "I didn't even know you and Kellin were dating."

Sibylla smiled. "We wanted to keep it to ourselves until we knew it was something."

Mikael shook Kellin's hand in an enthusiastic handshake. "Congratulations" they said earnestly to each other.

"Dad! This is awesome. Welcome to the family," Rolland said to Sibylla with a strong hug. Rolland was beaming.

"You look happy, Rolland," said Connor.

"I'm actually thrilled," said Rolland. "My father will no longer be alone. I feared he'd never recover from the loss of my mother whom he'd loved since childhood. It looks like he's finally ready to move on.

"I really like Sibylla. She brings out the best in my dad. They banter incessantly. They're so entertaining to watch. She makes my dad want to do things other than bury himself in his work. But they're also a great team at work." Kellin, Sibylla, and Olivia suddenly joined Connor and Rolland. Rolland took Olivia's hand and winked.

"Dad, Mom," he winked at Sibylla, "may I introduce you to your new daughter and granddaughter?" He put his arm around a pregnant Olivia to pull her forward. Olivia pulled out a chain around her neck. On it was a diamond engagement ring. Wait. It also had a matching wedding ring.

Sibylla hugged both newlyweds. Once the shock subsided, Kellin hugged his son and daughter-in-law. Olivia mumbled something about facing death giving one the clarity to act on one's priorities.

Olivia, Dania, and Sibylla fell into a girls-only conversation while the three men compared notes on their courtships.

Olivia said, "I finally lost patience with how long Rolland was taking to propose and interrupted him with a loud 'Yes!' I pulled him up off his knee and kissed him."

Rolland overheard and went beet red right to the tips of his ears as he beamed at his new wife with a smile. Others in the room came over to shake the hands of the two husbands-to-be and to congratulate the newlyweds.

Someone screamed. It was Freya. Axl was writhing on the floor. "Help my husband, Freya" shouted hysterically. "Help. Help. Please save him. You must save him." Many rushed to surround Minister Dahl.

"Could it be a heart attack?" asked someone in the group.

"It looks more like an epileptic fit," suggested another.

"No, No," said Freya. "He doesn't have epilepsy."

"Could this be strychnine poisoning?" asked Dania. "Could someone have poisoned the Supreme Commander?" she asked as she called him by his old title in error in her panic. As with the masses, Dania still emotionally felt that Minister Dahl was the true Supreme Commander of Annutia.

Supreme Commander Riis was not popular and growing less so daily. At worst, he was viewed as malevolent, dishonest, and the worst of what politicians can be. At best, he was viewed as an incompetent lame duck, or worse, a puppet for big money.

"What do you know about poisoning, Dania?" asked Kane of the astrobiologist as he knelt over Axl to hold his shoulders to prevent injury from his rapid convulsions.

"The first sign of exposure is the body's muscles spasming like this. They start with the head and neck. The spasms then spread to every muscle in the body with nearly continuous convulsions. The convulsions progress, increasing in intensity and frequency until the backbone arches continually. Death comes from asphyxiation caused by paralysis of the neural pathways that control breathing, or from exhaustion due to the convulsions. Death occurs within two to three hours after exposure."

"Where was Axl three hours ago?" demanded Connor gently of Freya.

"He was at the Council meeting. All the ministers and their wives were there."

Both Connor and Lenore had listened intensely to Dania's information.

Connor!" Lenore commanded. "Bring me a large container from the bar half filled with water. Bring me something with which to stir." Lenore rushed to the fireplace, grabbed the shovel next to the poker from the fireplace implements, and began to smash the charcoal to ash and cinder.

Meanwhile, Connor sped to the bar and filled the largest container with water – a crystal martini pitcher with a long glass stirrer. He rushed to Lenore's side on the hearth to help her scoop the crushed charcoal into the pitcher.

While there, Lenore took the opportunity to speak to Connor confidentially. In a lowered voice, she said, "I didn't want to say this in front of Freya but, given the previous attempts on Axl's life, I'm going to treat this as a poisoning."

"I figured as much," said Connor quietly. "I think we're both thinking of that movie we watched recently for my murder mystery obsession whereby a victim had to be saved from poisoning. Connor began stirring vigorously. In a flash they were both back to Axl convulsing on the floor. Lenore immediately took charge. She knew exactly what to do.

"Connor, raise his head," requested Lenore.

"I brought this as well," Connor said as he handed Lenore a crystal funnel from the bar. She grabbed Axl's chin and began pouring the charcoal mixture down his throat using the funnel. It took five minutes, but the Minister's body gradually began to sag into the floor in exhaustion. The convulsions were over. The charcoal had been effective.

While she worked, Lenore tried to comfort Freya. "We're giving Axl charcoal to keep any swallowed poisons from being absorbed from his stomach into his bloodstream," explained Lenore to Freya. The solution to most poisonings is the infusion of an activated charcoal slurry.

While he worked, Connor took the time to contemplate the larger context of this situation to assess the danger to the three Earthlings. Axl was their protector. He was the only one they could trust to return them to Earth. Many of his enemies and detractors disliked Connor's program. There was real danger for them if he died. This was the fourth attempt on the Minister's life in as many days.

But more than this, Axl was his friend. He loved and admired this most impressive man. He was the heart of the Annutia. He would always be their Supreme Commander. Connor was extremely distressed by this situation.

Medics had been called but had not yet arrived. No sooner was Axl resting peacefully than another cacophony arose from one of the many vignettes of couches. It was the towering Defense Minister, Karsten Kolbeck, who had been felled next to a large leather couch. His convulsions took the same form as what they had witnessed with Axl.

"Connor! Water!" said Lenore as she headed back to the fireplace again.

"I have it already," said Daniel as he followed her to the fireplace. No sooner had they attended to Minister Kolbeck than Commander-in-Chief Trygg succumbed as well.

Connor immediately got on the phone to alert Birgitte to the exposure at the Council meeting. "I'll contact the Poison Commission to enlist their help," said Axl's executive assistant.

Luminary Ozias went down next. Then Annalise was down. Daniel was immediately by her side with a cocktail shaker of water in preparation for a charcoal slurry. He looked around the room and saw that Lenore was still busy.

"Connor," Daniel called. "Charcoal. It's Annalise."

As Connor dashed to the fireplace, the Azurite Chief of State, Einar Nyhus, bolted to Annalise's side at speeds unexpected for the diplomatic stature he normally presented. He immediately held her shoulders to minimize the effects of the spasms wracking her body.

"Hold on, Annalise. Help is coming. It'll be alright," he soothed. The Minister called to his assistant standing immobilized by shock.

"Call my driver to the front entrance." The assistant pressed a speed dial on his phone and ordered the driver.

Daniel assumed that Nyhus was simply caring for a fellow Azurite. They were both black with electric blue eyes. There was no denying their shared heritage. But there was an unexpected intimacy or familiarity in his demeanor.

Connor was back at the fireplace for charcoal. He quickly rushed back to Daniel with a shovel full of charcoal. Daniel covered the cocktail shaker and shook it to mix the charcoal slurry.

"Hold her head up," Connor instructed the Azurite leader as Daniel began pouring the mixture into the funnel in her mouth to counteract the poison in her stomach. As she relaxed, Nyhus swept her up in his arms.

"Freya," he called as he passed by her next to the recovering Axl on the floor. "We're going to the hospital. Do you want Axl to come or are you waiting for the paramedics?"

"Oh, Yes. We'll come," said Freya gratefully as she stood up. Daniel and Connor immediately slung Axl's arms around their necks to help him up and to walk him to the car.

Freya spotted Lenore nearby giving a charcoal slurry to KahlDahr Chief of State Lennart Lorenson.

Thank you for saving my husband, Lenore," she called.

"Of course," said Lenore.

"Thank you," stammered Axl in gratitude for their having saved his life. His eyes were closed and his head hung forward because he was still too exhausted to hold it upright. Connor understood what his friend was trying to say. They had reciprocated their kidnapping with kindness to their kidnapper and exploiter. Axl recognized that a special bond had formed beyond Stockholm syndrome between the abductees and their abductor.

At the elevator Daniel said to Einar, "I can come with her instead."

"No need," said the Chief of State. Annalise is my wife. Something in his expression suggested he knew of young Daniel's obvious infatuation with his wife. With his usual diplomacy, he allowed Daniel to save face by continuing, "Your security team would not be pleased with me for extracting you from this building, Daniel."

Two of Einar's security team took over, shouldering Axl into the elevator. As Einar stepped into the elevator still carrying Annalise, he shouted for someone to take her. He fell to the elevator floor in convulsions. Daniel and Connor stood by helplessly in horror as the elevator door closed. Seconds later, two sets of elevator doors burst open taking the two by surprise. Four paramedics emerged with two gurneys.

"Azurite Chief of State just exited the elevator in the lobby. He needs a charcoal slurry," ordered Connor anxiously.

Two paramedics are with Nyhus and his wife now in an ambulance going to the hospital. Activated charcoal will be administered to the Minister en route.

"Excellent. Please come this way," directed Connor as he led them to Lenore. Lenore had now funneled charcoal into nine of the twelve Ministers. She immediately began to update the lead paramedic as to the symptoms and what she'd done. The other three began attending to the Ministers lying powerlessly in exhaustion on the various couches or rich Bokhara carpets on the floor.

The lead paramedic responded to Lenore's summary. "These symptoms are similar to what people all over the planet have been experiencing due to algae neurotoxin poisoning. In high enough concentrations, the water treatment filtration systems became unable to remove the toxins completely. After a year, we routinely carry kits of activated charcoal to do exactly what you've done. Your quick action saved our planetary government today, Lenore. Thank you!"

He used a walkie talkie to let his fellow paramedics know what he suspected. He continued speaking to Lenore and Connor, "If the Ministers ate shellfish or any of those species of fish, animals and birds which are higher up the food chain, the accumulation of toxins may have reached extremely concentrated levels. Scientists are estimating that at the worst point more than 70% of our food chain was tainted and 100% of our water." The paramedic moved away to attend to the Ministers.

"What a scary thought," shuddered Lenore.

Instantly, Connor was on his phone again to Birgitte at Axl's office to update her. "Birgitte, what food was served to the Ministers today? Nothing potentially toxic about that. Could you please check the date on the water provided for today's Council meeting?" He flicked the phone onto speaker mode so Lenore could hear.

"I'll be back to you in a minute, Commander Kane."

"Sir, the water is dated this month."

"Are you sure it's properly treated with the new filtration system that Henerik Halderson had developed to protect people from the algae?"

Within seconds Birgitte cried, "Oh no, Commander. It's from this month last year." Neither could speak for a moment with this chilling news. So many died from toxic water a year ago.

"I'll leave this in your capable hands to resolve, Birgitte. Axl, Annalise, and Einar have been taken to the hospital by ambulance. Perhaps you could locate them and let their doctors know."

"Yes sir. Thank you," she said relieved that he made no judgement of her mistake or accidental complicity in the contamination.

"How is Minister Dahl? How are the other Ministers?"

"It's really touch-and-go at the moment, Birgitte. The first 24 hours are critical. We'll have to see if they make it through the night. We can only hope that the charcoal was in time to absorb the toxins in their stomachs."

When he hung up, Connor began to consider some rather suspicious elements about this poisoning that suggested that it was deliberate. Why would the two "unpoisoned" Ministers have wanted to get rid of the others?

"Annalise is married!" interrupted Daniel shaking his head in disbelief.

"When I think about it, it makes sense," said Connor. There's something similar in their manner beyond race. Heroic, fearless, kind, compassionate, world-centric, altruistic. They're both strong and talented diplomats dedicated to helping humanity."

"I never suspected," said Daniel shaking his head. "I saw no evidence. Not even a ring. She never said."

"They probably had to keep it a secret for Annalise to be taken seriously in her work. I had to do the same for Lenore. She is her own person with her own significant expertise and talent. She doesn't deserve to be downplayed or typecast as simply my wife. People made the wrong assumptions any time she was standing next to me.

"Daniel, why would the two 'unpoisoned' Ministers have wanted to get rid of the others? Supreme Commander Rikard Riis and Pieter Holst, the Minister-in-Charge of the Pharmaceuticals Coalition?"

22
THE BREAK-INS

Rolland and his security guard, Bjarne, waited within the glass doors to Bergh Renewable Resources Inc. as usual at 7:00 p.m. at the end of his allotted workday. If he hadn't promised Olivia he'd be home for dinners, Rolland would happily live with his algae farming work 24/7. His dad was the same. They were unapologetic workaholics.

Rolland's driver pulled up in his bulletproof prestige car. Bjarne pulled out his gun and stepped outside to survey the terrain. He waved Rolland outside.

Rolland called "Good Night, Rikter" to the security guard at the front desk.

"Good night, Mr. Bergh," called Rikter, the reception security guard.

The two entered the backseat of the car and the driver pulled ahead along the large circular drive. Rolland always liked to look back at the complex to enjoy what he and his dad had built. Within a few months his whole world and his prospects had changed beyond anything he'd imagined.

"Stop!" yelled Rolland unexpectedly. He'd turned off the lights of his offices and those of Mikael and Dania for the BioVari satellite offices. Yet he was now seeing three flashlights moving through both. "Take us back to the front door," Rolland commanded. "Bjarne, look at the three flashlights in the third-floor offices."

Bjarne immediately dialed the police so as not to take any chances. He texted other personnel to alert them to the break-in. He told the driver to pull away to the side of the building once they had disembarked.

Rolland texted Kellin, Mikael and Dania to suggest they orchestrate whatever else was necessary. He would keep them informed. Rolland and Bjarne then jumped out of the car and used the two access monitors to scan their hands simultaneously for entry into the building. There was no one at the front desk which was against protocol.

Could something have happened to Rikter? Was he complicit? Was he helping someone to the confidential inventions and formulas those offices held? Rolland flung himself behind the security desk to view the situation from the various screens and systems.

"Stay there, Rolland," commanded Bjarne. Hide under the desk or in the Security Room if anyone comes."

"The metal grid gates are open," Rolland shouted after Bjarne as the man was running into the stairwell. Rolland immediately closed the grid gates so that the most critical documents, safes, and computer systems were protected. Suspiciously, the third-floor cameras had been turned off. He switched them on again and made sure they were recording. Someone was copying material from the decoy computer. Rolland assumed there would be repercussions in the coming weeks.

Rolland sent out a break-in alert to the building security forces but no one responded. Where was everyone? Had they been taken hostage? Or worse? When Rolland heard the elevators moving towards the lobby, he quickly ducked under the security desk out of view. He took the video monitor for the lobby camera with him so he could see what was happening.

The lobby camera had also been turned off. Rolland turned it back on and ensured they were recording. Three hooded men in black walked quickly through the lobby to the front door. One was on some kind of communication device.

"The operation might have failed," he said. "You'll have to extract the material from the Government Complex. The BioVari Head Office mission is a go. The residence mission is a go."

"Heard and heard, sir!" came back the response.

When they'd left the building, Bjarne exited from the stairwell to meet up with Rolland. "I think I closed the grid gates in time. The thieves were blocked from extracting anything of value."

When Rolland explained that the head offices of BioVari were next, Bjarne sprang into action. He redirected the police and security to not just protect those offices but to set a trap for the pending robbers. They could then be interrogated for their employer in trade for a lighter sentence.

Mikael called at that moment, so Rolland answered to bring him up to date. They agreed to meet up at the Government Complex for the capture if Security would allow. "I'm so glad Commander Kane told us how to legally and physically protect ourselves. I'm sure Dahl Enterprises will be ready to dispute any patent infringements," said Mikael.

Bjarne and Rolland then set off to search the building to locate the security guards. They found them alive and well all-tied-up in the first floor Security Room. All except for Rikter who sits at the front desk. This was obviously an inside job. Was it also going to be an inside job at the Government Complex as well? Who could be the mastermind behind this?

Mikael's and Dania's genetically engineered algal viruses and benign algae were worth millions in the hands of the Bergh's algae synergy systems complex, especially those for the biofuels and minerals like lithium that could be mined.

However, the attempted theft was undoubtedly as much for the BioVari creations as for how we're commercializing them. Their genetic engineering wouldn't be half as profitable without the model we're using to create synergy among various algae applications. Both parts are needed to duplicate their lucrative revenue streams.

My dad and Jordaan Jostad had a brilliance for interlinking all the equipment and processes for a simplicity and economy of operation that is unprecedented. Nothing is wasted, redundant, or duplicated, including within Olivia's computer systems. All of the various operations are as compressed as possible. Production is extremely efficient with very little wastage on any process.

♦ ♦ ♦

Service for the court case followed. Surely, they weren't this stupid thought Rolland. It was one week after the break-ins that BioVari and Bergh Renewable Resources received the documentation for a legal claim for all profits to date and for all future profits for the various inventions which others claimed they invented. Holst Pharmaceuticals. Minister Holst's family company. Isn't it interesting that Pieter Holst, the Minister-in-Charge of the Pharmaceuticals

Coalition, was one of the two survivors of the Council poisonings?

The thieves had been caught red-handed as they attempted to breach the BioVari Head Offices in the Government Complex. They must have been paid a lot because they refused to reveal who hired them. The copy of the decoy material was never recovered. The insider who had let them in was never identified.

The Dahl lawyers will have this cleaned up in the first court session thought Rolland with delight. The Commander ensured that we'd be ready for this. We've outsmarted them! They're going down!

23
THE COURT CASE

"This is a hearing to determine whether we need a trial," explained Judge Nykvist, "and, if so, what kind of trial. Are there probable causes that a crime or crimes have been committed or just civil disputes between or among businesses?

I will hear a summary of the arguments and evidence from the Plaintiffs, Holst Pharmaceuticals, and then the same from the Defendants, Dahl Enterprises, BioVari Inc., and Bergh Renewable Resources.

"Rebuttals can follow but no interruptions of these case summaries with arguments, please. This is a hearing not a trial. You don't need to try to influence me with your ability to argue or your outrage at what is being presented by your opponents.

"I note that the Defendants have countersued. In addition, they've requested a Summary Judgement to terminate the Plaintiffs' case based on their extensive documented evidence. I won't address this until after the summaries."

It would appear that Annutian court procedure is quite current with the trend in the U.S. to replace grand juries with adversarial preliminary hearings to determine the necessity of trials noted Connor.

The Plaintiffs' lawyer stood up. Hakon Kron began by trying to impress the Judge by introducing Pieter Holst, the Minister-in-Charge of the Pharmaceuticals Coalition. He explained that before assuming office and on the advice of counsel, Minister Holst had resigned his position as CEO of Holst Pharmaceuticals, a family business which generates over 80% of global pharmaceutical sales.

Judge Nykvist welcomed the Minister deferentially as was required by protocol. However, it was apparent that Judge Nykvist was neither impressed with planetary royalty nor the man himself.

Hakon Kron continued. The Plaintiffs were apparently claiming ownership of all the innovations and creations that Dania and Mikael had developed and all of the ingenious implementation processes of the Berghs. Because of these alleged thefts of intellectual property on the part of the creatives, the Plaintiffs felt that the millions of dollars in past profits and profits of the future were due to Holst Pharmaceuticals. In addition to patent infraction, they wanted to lay criminal charges as well for the thefts of intellectual property.

Dania's face displayed dismay, outrage, and fear. Connor motioned to her to shrug it off and regain quiet repose. All would be alright.

The Plaintiffs presented evidence that could only have been acquired during the break-ins of the Defendants' offices and residences. How wise of Judge Nykvist to have admonished no interruptions. The Defendants were about to hang themselves.

Hakon Kron continued with the direct examinations of a variety of scientists who affirmed that the documentation proved that the inventions came from the long-standing projects at Holst Pharmaceuticals. They provided patents dating back over a year.

"Thank you for the Plaintiffs' summary," said the Judge perfunctorily to the Plaintiffs' lawyer. He then nodded to the Defendants' lawyer, Tate Storr.

Connor well knew how impressive the inventions and breakthroughs tended to be when his savanting protocol was used. Harnessing and exploiting the bioflow can yield incredible flashes of genius. After a career in the breakthrough business, these kinds of court cases were simply business as usual for Connor Kane. Someone is always seeking to steal hard work and creativity which was not theirs.

He was delighted that it was now time to reap the benefits of the methods he'd pressured the creatives to use to protect their inventions from the inevitable thieves. He always enjoyed the justice of it all. The defeat of the Goliaths by the Davids.

Tate Storr began the Defendants' case by introducing the Breakthru Mission and what was behind the world-saving breakthroughs on the part of everyone in the program.

"The Defendants had filed patents which were approved because experienced individuals in the Annutia Patent Agency did not find them in conflict with any existing patents. Since the Plaintiffs are claiming prior Patents, this led us to question their evidence.

"We ask Your Honor to review the written and video diaries in Chambers for the development of each invention by the Defendants. These were provided to the court not 24 hours after this suit was filed to demonstrate that there was not enough time in which they could've been fabricated.

"I'll take this under advisement," responded the Judge.

"We object, Your Honor," said the Defendants' lawyer, Hakon Kron. We should be able to review the defendants' documentation as well.

"We object," said the Defendants' lawyer in response. "I think this is precisely what the Plaintiffs have been trying to accomplish in filing this court case, Your Honor. We find it rather suspicious that their Claim application comes 1 week after break-ins to the Defendants' residences and offices in which attempts were made to source this exact same information. We ask that Your Honor not reward this misuse of the justice system until the necessity and nature of a trial is determined and underway. "

"Sustained," said Judge Nykvist to the Defendants' objection. "Again, I ask that the summaries progress without interruption or argument."

Dania smiled at Mikael. Finally, some good news.

"These videotapes and documentation track every step of the development of the BioVari formulas. Even if these formulas were proven to be the same as those of the Plaintiffs would not that give the Defendants ownership of the profits from the Plaintiffs?

"Alternatively, they would simply highlight that a patent was issued in error. Inevitable discovery by others with normal knowledge of the same field makes the invention unpatentable. Thus, their patents cannot be upheld. Ownership by the Plaintiffs could no longer be proven."

"Further, it would not have been possible for our Defendants to have read and copied the Plaintiffs' patents, because they didn't exist until the break-ins. I would like to approach to present a copy of patent documentation to Your Honor and the Plaintiffs.

"Come ahead," said Judge Nykvist.

"This evidence shows that the patent numbers, which the Plaintiffs claim they developed over a year ago, belong to other inventions not those of the Plaintiffs. This suggests that the Plaintiffs had help from inside the Annutia Patent Agency to fabricate this hoax for your Court today, Your Honor.

"As I understand it, Your Honor, your assignment to this case was last minute. There is a possibility that this hoax was meant to work with help from one of your colleagues on the bench."

The Judge scowled at this breach of courtroom etiquette in disparaging one of his colleagues. Connor suspected that Tate Storr had decided ahead of time to say what needed to be said and apologize afterwards if necessary. Consequently, the Judge's disapproval had no effect whatsoever on his calm matter-of-fact presentation of their very substantial evidence.

"In the evidence we've provided Your Honor, you'll find a copy of the original patents for the patent numbers and dates that the Plaintiffs are claiming for their own patents in order to suggest that their patents pre-date those of the Defendants.

"Therefore, should they implement based on the patents of the Defendants, it is the Plaintiffs' profits which would actually belong to my clients not the other way around as claimed."

The Plaintiffs guffawed. Connor noticed that Dania smiled at Mikael and squeezed his hand.

"In addition, Your Honor, the patent documentation placed into the file numbers of other patents isn't valid. It could never have yielded the results achieved by my clients in saving the planet from the repercussions of the algae invasion.

"As part of their very dedicated effort to protect their discoveries and inventions, they created decoy materials on less protected computers. It is with these decoy materials that the Plaintiffs have chosen to pretend that they could have generated the results and profits of the Defendants.

"Rather than filing these decoy fabricated materials with the Annutia Patent Agency, we thought it more prudent to file them with the Annutia Copyright Agency. We wanted to be able to prove our authorship of what the Plaintiffs are claiming is theirs.

"Your Honor, if I may, I would like to approach to provide you and the Plaintiffs with this copyright filing, so you may see it is identical to the patents the Plaintiffs have claimed to have filed. This was the material taken in the break-in and thus proves the Plaintiffs were behind that break-in. Therefore, in addition to the offences inherent in this evidence, there should be criminal charges for the break-ins from which the Plaintiffs sourced these materials.

"Please approach," invited the Judge.

After comparing the copyright filing with the patent filings, Judge Nykvist looked disapprovingly at the Plaintiffs' lawyer who was making the same comparison. Hakon Kron blanched. It was apparent to everyone that he'd been duped by his clients. He was neither informed nor complicit.

Tate Storr continued with more layers of the Plaintiffs' offences. "Unfortunately, the Plaintiffs have made a silly mistake in not vetting their so-called patented formulas. This then calls into question, all of the expert witnesses who have testified in this Court today, Your Honor. Assuming they have the credentials that they claim, they have lied under oath to defraud the Court and the Defendants. At minimum, perjury charges need to be laid.

"Further, Your Honor, the Holst Pharmaceuticals patents not only don't work because they are decoys, they would never have been approved. I have a geneticist and patent lawyer and other patent experts here whom I can call upon to testify about the vagueness of the patent which would have made it impossible for patent approval.

"For example, on page 22 of the patent, paragraph 3, you'll see that this fake patent impacts 50% of the genes identified in the algae genome. Obviously, the

Plaintiffs had no idea which genes were relevant to the work done by BioVari and they still don't. It's unlikely that our vague decoy material would have met the specificity requirements for approval by the Annutia Patent Agency.

"In addition, we were facing a planetary disaster. Holst Pharmaceuticals were given billions of dollars to save the planet. If their patents existed and worked from their false filing dates, they would have been contractually obligated to quickly make the algae benign and create an algae farming and processing complex as Bergh Renewable Resources have done as BioVari's implementation partner.

"They then should have spread these complexes across the planet. The Plaintiffs either didn't have the patents they claim, or they defrauded the government of billions of dollars in research money by not applying those patents to the crises faced by the planet.

"Given the dates on their claimed patents, they would have had a year to apply those patents to solve the life-threatening challenges. They didn't do that even though they were obligated to do so based on the contracts surrounding their receipt of government funding.

"My clients eliminated the bulk of the toxic algae plague and its repercussions within a few months of their discoveries. Why did the Plaintiffs not do the same?" Connor noticed that Dania was now enjoying the court case. She was smiling. Mikael was smiling. Kellin and Rolland were smiling. He was smiling.

"The Berghs' implementation model also doesn't have any precedent since the algae are new to this planet. Their procedures have thus been patented as well. The Plaintiffs have no such patents for their implementation process of their supposed BioVari duplicate formulas.

"My clients left no decoy materials for what Bergh Renewable Resources had developed. Thus, the Plaintiffs cannot prove they could have implemented the BioVari patents to generate the profits they feel are owed to them.

"To reiterate, Judge Nykvist, by not implementing solutions if they supposedly had the means, they are admitting to taking government grants under false pretenses. The Plaintiffs thus have the choice (a) to admit to fraud in taking government grants; and/or (b) to admit to fraud in the evidence they have presented today; and/or (c) to admit to theft in trying to steal these patents from the homes and offices of my clients."

Connor noticed that Hakon Kron's shoulders had drooped. His arrogant air had been replaced by embarrassment at his not having done his due diligence.

"Collusion with government patent agents to change patent information with the intent to defraud obviously also needs to be investigated. And I believe additional criminal charges need to be laid, Your Honor, in 11 counts of attempted murder of 10 Ministers and Annalise Nyhus. I would like to submit some additional evidence to back up my accusation."

Judge Nykvist waved Storr forward. The look of neutrality on Nykvist's face had been replaced by horror at the magnitude of the wrongdoings he hadn't expected from today's proceedings.

"The police gathered the water bottles from the Council Chamber as evidence right after the poisoning. The water was bottled a year ago during a time when filtration could not remove algae neurotoxins. Thousands died back then. The serial numbers on the bottles of toxic water used for these attempted murders had been allotted to the Holst's Pharmaceuticals labs for experimentation purposes in solving the challenges of the algae plague.

"Only two ministers were not poisoned, Supreme Commander Rikard Riis and his long-time friend, Minister Pieter Holst, former CEO of the family-owned Holst Pharmaceuticals and Minister-in-Charge of the Pharmaceuticals Coalition. This is a good direction into which the police homicide division might select for investigation. Normally both Ministers take coffee for the Council meetings. But, at this last meeting, they both abstained.

"I object to these slanderous accusations," declared Kron. "I request that they be stricken from the record."

"Overruled," said the Judge sharply.

"Constable, I order an immediate investigation into the accusations of Defense Counsel. If these poisonings have been deliberate, the perpetrators need to be identified and brought to justice. The officer acknowledged the Judge's orders.

"First," said Judge Nykvist, "I would like to thank the Defendants and the other creatives for your incredible service to Annutia and all Annutians. We might not even be here today without you. May I also say that I am truly impressed with the extent of the evidence and the preparedness of the Defendants. This certainly makes my job easier.

"Mr. Kron, do the Plaintiffs have any explanation for this situation or any rebuttals to the evidence of the Defendants?"

The Plaintiffs' lawyer was crestfallen. It was obvious that Kron had not known about his clients' subterfuge.

"Not at this time, Your Honor."

"Am I right in assuming that the Plaintiffs will be dropping this suit? Do you wish that order?" asked the Judge of the Plaintiff's lawyer.

Kron turned to view the faces of the members of the Plaintiffs party beside and behind him.

"We do, Your Honor," answered the Plaintiff's lawyer.

"So ordered."

"May we take the Plaintiffs into custody for interrogation, Your Honor?" asked the Bailiff. Four police constables stood up by the back door of the courtroom to stop members of the Plaintiffs party attempting to flee the courtroom.

Judge Nykvist ordered all Plaintiffs to accompany the four police officers.

Two individuals stood up whose dark suits and clean-cut looks suggested government agents. "Your Honor, I'm Special Prosecutor Gerlach Grahn from the Global Security Agency, the GSA. The Defendants have provided us with the evidence you've heard today. Since this case involves the attempted murder of members of the Annutia Planetary Steering Council, we believe this matter is better investigated by the GSA. We have agents prepared to take the Plaintiffs in this room into custody. Warrants for other individuals are currently being served. We ask your permission to proceed."

"I agree. So ordered," said Judge Nykvist.

And that was that. Kane had wanted each of his creatives to receive the wealth and acclaim to which they were due for their invention and creativity. Not only because they deserved it, but because their wealth would move them into positions of planetary power.

They would be in a position to imprint the cultural changes they'd undergone with savanting onto an entire planet.

A power shift to a talent-driven society in which discriminations and conflicts could ultimately disappear would be possible. With the number of millionaires or soon-to-be millionaires within his creatives, Kane was well on his way to causing this world transformation that he and Axl sought. These were the new heroes to which everyone would aspire.

24
THE RE-INVASION

Mikael, Kellin, and Connor sat uncomfortably in the lavish seating area of the massive office of the Supreme Commander. With Rikard Riis in prison as a co-conspirator to the Council poisonings, Axl Dahl was the overwhelming voted choice of the masses for his replacement. For Dahl, there was no more desirable encore.

The Annutia Planetary Steering Council has since rescinded the rule for mandatory retirement of any Minister after two terms of five years. Most countries on the planet already allowed leaders to continue as long as the majority of voters wished. It was time for the Council to follow suit.

Connor began, "Supreme Commander, the creatives have some Annutia-shattering news about the algae that is both good and bad." Connor was surprised at his inadvertent flip of the term "earth-shattering". It was as if he'd just realized that he'd become one of them.

"Kellin with his algae farms and plants and Mikael as a microbiologist specializing in algae have arguably the greatest knowledge of algae on the planet. Mikael, could you please reveal your shocking discoveries?"

Mikael cleared his throat nervously. He may have saved the planet but he was still just a young man of 24 unaccustomed to communicating with authority figures. "Supreme Commander, while we've modified the algae to remove their toxicity, they are currently growing at such breakneck speeds that they are again clogging our waterways. They will shortly begin slowing the production of hydropower and blocking water filtration.

"There are literally blankets of algae blooms covering our lakes and rivers. They are blocking out the sunlight needed by many underwater plants and animals. This kills life up the food chain.

"When Dania and I walked the shores between the farms and the river and tested soil samples, we discovered why. The algae plague was caused by nutrient loading from farm runoff not xenoforming by extraterrestrials. The phosphorous and nitrates in fertilizers and sewage draining from the farms into the river are algae superfood that has drastically accelerated their growth.

"Chemicals and manure designed to nourish crops wash into our lakes, streams and oceans to provide a nutrient-rich buffet for algae. Add to this nice warm thermal pollution from power plants and factories also along the waterways. This puts the algae into high-growth heaven.

"The toxic algae plague was indeed an invasion but not of the otherworldly sort. It was homegrown. *We* have been destroying our planet. *We* are the enemy.

"The gases the algae emit displace the oxygen from the water so that there are dead spots where animals and plants can no longer exist. The expansion of these dead spots could potentially eliminate the lower rungs of the food chain with repercussions up the ladder.

"This is indeed shocking news," said Axl, his usual unperturbable facade visibly shaken. "I never wanted my people to have to go through such crises again. Yet here we are. I see now, Commander Kane, why the bioflow was not supporting your creatives working on the attack of Miasma or off-planet colonization. What are your recommendations, Mikael?"

"Immediate action is obviously required," urged Mikael. "The laws we've set up for other industries with regard to polluting waterways need to extend to agriculture. We need to be as strict with the regulation of wastewater from farms as we are for the treatment of waste from a pulp and paper mill, a foundry, a cannery, or a sewage plant.

"The Agricultural Faction is massive and powerful on Annutia," Axl explained. "They'll fight us tooth and nail." Axl sighed already exhausted in the face of the pending fight. "But this is the work of politicians not you. What specifically do we need, Mikael?"

"We recommend that Annutia make anti-pollution methods mandatory with strict censures. These censures need to have teeth – fines, imprisonment, loss of licenses, a boycott of products produced in ways that threaten the environment, and so on. These are essential to save our planet from repeating Miasma's fate.

"We need restrictions as to what types of fertilizers can be used. Dramatic reductions in synthetic fertilizers is recommended. No more destructive industrial nitrogen-fertilizer-laden and glyphosate-heavy agriculture, for example.

"There needs to be a 50-foot vegetation buffer around public waterways to prevent the accidental drainage of fertilizers. We can then visibly see that buffer from helicopters in order to police compliance. We need better specifications as to what human waste or sewage can be drained or discarded into waterways.

We need better testing to enforce those specifications."

While Axl had regained his façade, Connor could sense the stress of someone not knowing how to solve a desperate situation. Ever the politically savvy strategist, Connor interjected with a smile to break the drama.

"Are you above blackmail, Supreme Commander? You'll be wielding the necessary power if you threaten to expose the Agricultural Faction as the culprits who caused the recent planetary crises. The threat to publish the pictures of Miasma as the future of Annutia if the Agriculture Faction does not comply may be enough to induce their compliance."

"Excellent strategy, Commander Kane," said Axl with a sigh of relief. He would indeed have significant power with which to maneuver them.

"Subsidies could also entice farmers to experiment with new conservation methods to ward off toxic runoff and protect water quality," continued Mikael. "This could include strategies such as building artificial wetlands and underground 'bioreactors' to capture nutrients in drainage systems.

"They could experiment with natural methods and soil-regenerative techniques such as using cover crops, composting, livestock integration. and no-till methods to slow fertilizer and pesticide runoff."

"Thank you for bringing this world-changing information to my attention. I'll take care of this. Thank you on behalf of Annutians everywhere for your service, Mikael, Kellin and Commander."

With this, the Supreme Commander rose and with a sweep of his arm ushered them towards the door to terminate the meeting. He then stopped to consider something.

"Commander Kane, could you please stay behind with me to talk on other matters?" Connor nodded and moved back to his seat.

Axl remained at the door to ask Birgitte to arrange an emergency meeting immediately in his office with the leaders of the Agriculture Faction. He also asked to meet immediately with his head of publicity. "Please provide him with a complete set of the pictures from Miasma. Thanks, Birgitte." He closed the door.

"Connor, you and your team have accomplished so much more than I asked or expected. I feel I can release you back to Earth if that is your preference. I and many others would rather that the three of you stayed here permanently and made Annutia your home. You've been pivotal to resolving the greatest crises Annutia has ever faced just as you did for Earth.

"Rather than retiring you after your 10-year term as they did on Earth, we want to keep you doing what you love and what you do better than anyone else. We want you to continue with your encore performance of maximizing the human resources of our planet to benefit each citizen, their families, and all Annutians. What do you say? Will you stay?"

"The three of us just recently discussed this very decision, Axl. As much as we have thrilled to our work here, and care for so many wonderful people here, we love Earth and many who live on Earth. Therefore, regrettably we must decline your magnanimous offer as tempting as it might be. However, we would love for you and Freya to visit us any time."

"Thank you. We would like that," responded Axl with reservations written all over his face. Connor suspected that there were some major secrets around this that Axl would never reveal to him.

"I wanted to let you know that the Breakthru Mission will continue without you. Annalise and Kellin are going to do the heavy lifting and Marta is going to assist.

"Excellent. All savanting experts. Kellin is going to give up his machine heaven to do this? Was this your talent for persuasion at work, Axl? As a past victim, I know how good you are."

"I'm innocent," laughed Axl. "Kellin says he's become a growth addict. He needs to operate planetwide with the challenges of new systems to explore and create. Also, he liked the opportunities you gave him to teach others about his experiences and wants to do more of that. He feels his experience of living savanting all his life made him especially equipped to help the human resources of the planet transcend. That is what he wants to do."

"The man is fascinating, is he not, Axl?"

"Indeed," said Axl. There is another matter I need to talk to you about, Connor. I understand that Jostad, Sr. talked to you about buying the Annutian rights to your book, *Savanting*. I would feel better if the Annutia Planetary Steering Council owned those rights so that they could be distributed throughout the world to benefit all. I'm prepared to offer you a million U.S. dollars in cash delivered to your home with you.

"This is very generous, Minister."

"I think I probably owe you."

"I'm thinking the same thing," said Connor laughing. "I accept. Thank you, Axl."

"Before we part, I wanted to ask if we're related, Axl? I look like a younger version of you and Lenore greatly resembles Freya. I hope you're not our parents. I prefer to be Lenore's husband not her brother," Connor laughed again.

Axl smiled but said not a word. He stood up and man-hugged Connor goodbye.

"We wish we could clone you with all of your experiences intact. Unfortunately, we're not yet that advanced. You will be missed, Connor."

"Well, I think that might be the nicest thing anyone has ever said to me," joked Connor facetiously with a wide grin and a twinkle in his eye.

"Good luck with all of your future endeavors, Connor."

"To you as well, Axl," said Connor with a handshake.

Axl then turned his attention to his phone for an incoming text. The meeting was over. Connor left the office. He joined up with Brik in the foyer to head back to the residence. The mystery was obviously going to continue thought Connor with a sigh. Cloning. That's an interesting thought. Was Axl trying to tell him something between the lines that he was not allowed to talk about? Could we perhaps have just been created from the same DNA? Lenore too? Is that why Axl is being so secretive?

25
THE DEBRIEF

Connor woke up in his very own bed at home on Earth. However, he had absolutely no remembrance of the ride home. A quick bathroom trip revealed he had wobbly wormhole legs so he knew he'd made the trip. There was cold pizza, sandwiches, fruit, and carafes of ice water and hot tea on his night table. Thank goodness for Annutian thoughtfulness. They've obviously dealt with this situation before.

"Well, that just happened," joked Connor when Lenore finally woke up.

"They must have drugged us for the trip home," Lenore speculated.

"What's the last thing you remember?" asked Connor.

"The three of us having dinner last night? Daniel" cried Lenore. "I hope he's okay. They wouldn't have kept him, would they?"

Connor picked up his phone from the night stand and texted Daniel. "Okay?"

"Okay." came back Daniel's response. "Sleeping. . . . in your guest room," he added.

"Daniel's in our guest room sleeping," reported Connor.

"Wonderful," responded Lenore. Daniel had become family. With no children of her own, Lenore often focused her maternal feelings on Daniel.

They went silent in their reveries about all that had happened to them. They were glad to be home. Yet they missed their friends and shared mission on Annutia. They had returned to a post-retirement void.

At his retirement gala before being abducted, Connor had wished wholeheartedly that he might continue his work of maximizing the world's human resources. Who'd have thought he'd get his wish in such an unusual form?

As impossible as his wish had been, the bioflow had managed his encore. The bioflow had reached across the galaxies to another planet to sustain his own maximization around applying his strongest talents.

"Daniel has texted to ask if he might join us on our bedroom couch," Connor said to Lenore. "I suspect he wants to debrief and decompress just like we do."

"Absolutely," Lenore agreed. "Invite him to join. I doubt if any of us could make it down to the living room."

Daniel wobbled into their room in a long hooded fleece bathrobe over pajamas.

"Good morning all," he said jovially.

"Good morning, Daniel," smiled Lenore delighted that all three had made it back. "You're so brave to try walking. I actually crawled to the bathroom last time I was up."

Daniel hugged the wall with his entire body as he edged his way around the room. He then just let himself fall unceremoniously onto the couch in a stomach sprawl. Daniel fished from his pocket one of the sandwiches that had been left on his night table and ate hungrily. Fortunately, it had not been flattened by his oblivious fall.

"Obviously, the Annutians have 'wormholed' people to Earth before and knew what they needed," he said.

"We've got cold pizza if you'd prefer," offered Lenore.

"I already ate mine," said Daniel. It was delicious. I was voraciously hungry."

Connor continued his musings. He contemplated the framed photo that had been left on his night table by whom he didn't know. He suspected Axl was behind it. It was a picture of he and Lenore with Axl and Freya.

"It was interesting how evasive Axl was after I asked if we are related," he revealed to Lenore.

"Really?" exclaimed Lenore. "You actually asked him that?"

"I did. Shortly afterwards as part of our goodbyes he talked about wishing he could clone me in order to keep me and my experience on Annutia. He said that unfortunately their science was not advanced enough yet.

"My resonance flagged that as highly significant. Cloning could be another explanation for our similar appearance, couldn't it? Was that our relationship? Could Axl and I and you and Freya have been created from the same DNA? Were we descendants, familially related, or clones?"

"Could I see that picture?" asked Daniel rousing from his sleepy sprawl.

Rather than pitch the picture covered in glass in its expensive silver frame, Connor deftly snapped a shot of the photo with his phone and cast it to the large screen TV. He was rather pleased with himself as a non-tech. He needed a solution that did not involve moving his wobbly body and he'd found one.

"Notice how much I look like Axl and Lenore looks like Freya? And we all look like we belong to the same tribe?"

"You're right," agreed Daniel. "The resemblances are too coincidental to be happenstance."

"Do you think we could be clones?" asked Connor.

"How could that work?" asked Lenore suddenly snapping out of her deep engagement with her tablet.

Daniel considered. "Axl's older. You'd have to be his clone."

"Or both of you are clones," conjectured Lenore. "Maybe two of many . . . . ?"

"There are more of you! Well, that's a scary thought, old man," grimaced Daniel with a teasing glint in his eyes. Connor scoffed back at him good-naturedly.

"What if Axl knew you were his clone," speculated Lenore. "And he brought you to Annutia because he assumed he knew you even if he'd never met you because he knew himself. He knew you and he had similar talents and ambitions, but you had additional experience that he didn't have. He might have assumed you'd operate like him for the mission but better."

"This would be the ultimate delegation of work," laughed Connor. "I would love to have a clone to which to delegate." They all laughed.

"That would explain why Axl cares so much for you," suggested Lenore.

"It might also explain why such a moral and humane man as Axl thought he had the right to borrow us as Earth talent to solve his problems," added Daniel only partially hiding his anger.

"Hmmm," said Connor thoughtfully.

"If there are Annutian clones on Earth, then could it be that they terraformed the Earth rather than we terraformed Annutia?" considered Daniel a little shocked at having conceived of such a notion.

"Of all of the options, Connor, my resonance seems to favor the one where you and Axl are both clones created from the same DNA specimen," shared Lenore.

"I think my resonance agrees, Lenore, but that scares me. That would explain why we were orphans, though, wouldn't it?

Lenore nodded. "Axl's age and our being here on Earth would suggest that clones were placed here from elsewhere."

"Could we all be clones," asked Daniel. "Could we be a planet of clones? Maybe that's why they never found the missing link from apes to humans."

"Could everything we know about the origins of earth, life, and homo sapiens be wrong?" asked Connor. "Is it all terraforming and cloning? Was it never evolution?"

"Scary," said Daniel. "If it's true, how could it have happened?"

"If not evolution and not clones," proposed Lenore, "could humans have been descendants of aliens as so many conjectured after Von Däniken's breakthrough book *Chariots of the Gods*? The missing piece was the absence of proof of human life or at least intelligent life on other planets. We three have that now."

"I don't know this book," interrupted Daniel.

"It was a little before your time, Daniel. 1968." Lenore explained, "Von Däniken's theory is that we're the descendants of galactic pioneers who continued to teach early humans. He has collected a multitude of archaeological discoveries which he feels demonstrate two things.

"He makes the case that ancient structures and artifacts appear to represent higher technological knowledge than is presumed to have existed at the times they were manufactured. Von Däniken maintains that these artifacts were produced either by (a) extraterrestrial visitors or by (b) humans who learned the necessary knowledge from more advanced beings.

"Von Däniken tries to show that many archaeological discoveries suggest they were designed to help those travelling in spaceships or 'chariots of the gods' as he calls them.

"It couldn't have been the Annutians," exclaimed Daniel. If von Däniken is talking about spaceships as chariots, we know the Annutians don't fly."

"Annutians can fly," Connor corrected. However, they banned flying because the factions kept bombing each other and other such hostilities. However, they don't need to fly since wormholes connect Miasma, Annutia and Earth.

"Could the Miasmians have terraformed both Annutia and Earth using the same cocktail?" suggested Connor. "Could they have used the same DNA to launch both populations of humans?"

"Or was there another population providing DNA and terraforming to all three planets," chimed in Daniel.

"Annutia copies so much from Earth. I think they must have been created after us." reasoned Lenore.

Connor thought back over Earth history. "The Annutians seem to trace back to Earth in the 1960s. Could that be when the United States and Russia were threatening to nuke the planet and wipe out the human race? Maybe Annutia was terraformed and received identical cloned DNA for people which were activated as a backup to Earth destroying itself?

"Transporting the DNA of many could be accomplished with much smaller crafts than what would be required to transport all of the various kinds of people we have on Earth to have them procreate.

Babies could simply be birthed from supplied DNA and each race begun."

"Then where would Von Däniken's advanced knowledge have come from that is evident in the ancient civilizations?" questioned Lenore. "The Mayans, the Egyptians, the Greeks, and so on?

"Could the creators have learned to imbed this advanced knowledge in their clones?" speculated Daniel. "Memory engrams? Could that be why we see savants with damaged brains performing mental feats beyond their capabilities based on access to massive knowledge databases?"

"That would be an interesting alternative to my speculation on downloads from the bioflow's holographic database underpinning all of the universe and humanity," exclaimed Connor.

"Maybe human Earth clones were taken back along the wormhole or in spacecrafts to more advanced civilizations and then returned with more advanced knowledge. Maybe this is the true purpose of UFO abductions if there are such occurrences. Also, it would be understandable that creators would want to come back to visit their creations," hypothesized Lenore.

"Your idea that Annutia is a backup for when we inevitably destroy Earth, would seem to be supported by the fact that the Annutians know about us but we know nothing of them. This seems to reinforce your idea that the terraformers and cloners were trying to prevent the repeat of what they thought might be happening on Earth. They wanted to ensure that Annutia survived."

Lenore weighed in. "My resonance suggests that the Miasmians created both planets and that Annutia was the encore of Earth for the reasons you suggest. But also, to have backup for their own planet.

"I suspect the Miasmians knew they were destroying their planet but could not get it under control any more than Earth has done," surmised Daniel. "They are a cautionary tale for those on Earth and we are the cautionary tale for the Annutians."

"Wouldn't it be fabulous," exclaimed Lenore excitedly, if we found the entrance to the wormhole? Then we could go back to visit our family of creatives whenever we wanted? Wouldn't that be great?"

"Wonderful," said Daniel. No doubt with thoughts of Annalise or some other ladies he had cultivated over the last several months thought Connor. Actually, Daniel and Marta had been becoming friends.

Connor considered for a moment. "Maybe they haven't revealed the whereabouts of the entrance to the wormhole on Earth because they think we'll destroy their planet like we're destroying our own. Maybe people from Earth wouldn't be welcome on

Annutia. Annutia has learned from Earth's mistakes. This might explain Axl's secrecy."

"I hope that Earth will not be the repeat of Annutia's algae plague. Or worse. The wasteland planet of Miasma. This is an encore we could do without."

The three fell quiet as they considered some of the radical possibilities upon which they had speculated. How do you process living science fiction thought Connor?

26
DÉJÀ-VU

Daniel was sleeping on the couch. Lenore was deep into research on her tablet. Connor was flicking through the hundreds of phone messages and emails that had accumulated over the last several months. Lenore interrupted the silence.

"Connor, did you know about algae plagues here on Earth?" asked Lenore finally looking up from her deep dive on her tablet. Connor went white and stared at her. Daniel opened his eyes.

"Listen to these articles." She began reading out several algae plague headlines and story excerpts from all over the world dating back several decades. Daniel sat up.

"Did you know that most of the large cities along the Mediterranean Sea discharge all of their sewage into the sea untreated. The same is true for most coastal developing countries. This is superfood for algae. The resulting algae blooms are massive.

"It seems that no part of the world is immune. Here's a 2017 U.S. headline: '*Toxic algae: Once a Nuisance, now a Severe Nationwide Threat.*'[1] Within the past decade, outbreaks have been reported in every state, a trend likely to accelerate as climate change boosts water temperatures.'"[2] Lenore stopped speaking to continue reading to herself.

Daniel fished his phone out of his robe pocket and began to research himself.

"Here's a 2014 article that also says the invasion has spread across the US," said Daniel. "It's entitled '*It's not just Ohio — Poisonous Algae Blooms now Plague 20 US States.*'[3] He skimmed some more then summarized, "New York is hardest hit, then Kansas and Washington."

"This article says, 'Lake Erie had one of the biggest algae blooms on record in 2015," read Lenore. She continued to skim the article. "'It blanketed 300 square miles – the size of New York City.'"[4] After scanning the article she continued with another excerpt.

"'Each year, during the summer months, a combination of warm waters in the shallow lake's west end, along with sunny weather and phosphorus from sources such as commercial agricultural runoff, sewage and industry, results in a population explosion of cyanobacteria - producing what's known as a harmful algal bloom (HAB).

"Listen to this," interrupted Connor. "In 2014, 'an algae toxin described in military texts as being as lethal as a biological weapon forced a two-day tap water shutdown for more than 400,000 customers in Toledo.'[5]

"Apparently, the politicians on Earth are having the same problem with the agriculture factions as Axl faced on Annutia. This is from May 2018. 'At a recent conference, the mayor of Toledo pointed the blame for the continuing [algae] problem squarely at the Ohio Farm Bureau Federation, saying that lawmakers in the state were too intimidated by the group to support legislation to deal with the problem.

"It's probably the most powerful interest group in Ohio," Mayor Wade Kapszukiewicz said in an interview . . . . *Nutrient runoff* comes from sewage and other sources, but mostly from fertilizer and manure, which are especially high in phosphorus.'"[6]

"I see now why Axl was so concerned about having to fight the Agricultural Faction. Fortunately, he had a little more leverage than Earth's politicians. Axl won!"

"I've got that same article," said Daniel. "Did you see that section where it says a March 2018 study found evidence that algal blooms are not just a *consequence* of climate change but they're also a *source* of climate-warming emissions."

"I didn't," said Connor scanning down the article.

Daniel continued, "It says that 'the algae emit methane and CO2 into the atmosphere which dramatically increases the greenhouse effect . . . . perhaps causing more damage than burning fossil fuels.'

"Apparently, and this is a quote from one of the researchers' . . . . even small increases in harmful algal blooms could impact the atmosphere. Basically, a little increase [in algal blooms] could cause the greenhouse effect of lakes to increase 5 to 40 percent."

Connor responded, "So, it could be that the increase in the greenhouse effect on Annutia that they thought was due to having switched over to burning fossil fuels could actually have been the result of the algae.

"Could well be," said Daniel. "The same researcher says, 'If we take Lake Erie and change it and make it as green as the part around Toledo, then the carbon emissions from the lake increases two-and-a-half more times and the atmospheric impact is *equivalent to adding another seven million cars on the road.*'"

"Wow," said Lenore. "That's scary. I don't think Annutia knows this information."

"I don't either," said Daniel. "Wikipedia talks about harmful algal blooms (HABS) around the globe. 'Researchers have reported the growth of HABS in Europe, Africa and Australia. Those have included blooms on some of the African Great Lakes, such as Lake Victoria, the second largest freshwater lake in the world. India has been reporting an increase in the number of blooms each year.

"'In 1977, Hong Kong reported its first red tide. By 1987, they were getting an average of 35 per year. Additionally, there have been reports of harmful algal blooms throughout popular Canadian lakes such as Beaver Lake and Quamichan Lake.

"''Global warming and pollution are causing algal blooms to form in places previously considered "impossible" or rare for them to exist, such as under the ice sheets in the Arctic, in Antarctica, the Himalayan Mountains, the Rocky Mountains, and in the Sierra Nevada Mountains.'''[7]

"Gosh," gasped Lenore. "The threat is already worldwide and growing. Here's a 2010 article entitled '*Massive Algae Bloom Spreading Across Baltic Sea*.' It says that a potentially toxic algae bloom covered 377,000 square kilometers, an area larger than all of Germany,"[8] summarized Lenore.

"Here's a 2011 headline that reads '*Toxic seaweed on French coast sparks health fears*,'" read Connor. "This article says, 'Experts have warned that the algae pose a health risk as when it rots it produces hydrogen sylphide, which, if trapped under a seaweed crust and suddenly released, can prove as deadly as cyanide.'"[9]

"Apparently, these algae not only grow, they travel," said Lenore. "This headline says '*Killer Algae Migrates to California Coast – Mediterranean species found near San Diego*. A noxious species of killer algae that has destroyed marine life across thousands of acres of the Mediterranean seabed has now invaded a coastal lagoon near San Diego and threatens to spread swiftly unless the fast-growing pest can be controlled.'"[10]

"Shocking" said Connor. "Didn't you say that untreated phosphorous waste is being routinely dumped into the Mediterranean, Lenore? Now we find out that the algae living on this waste have migrated across the world to the U.S.?

"Our world is connected by major waterways along which algae plagues can travel. Earth has far more waterways than Annutia. Therefore, no place in this world will be safe. Even in the Arctic and Antarctica or the highest mountains. Isn't that what Wikipedia said, Daniel?"

"You are right," said Daniel with apprehension. Connor could see from Daniel's face that he had suddenly realized the connections that Connor was making.

Lenore got it at the same time and turned white. "We've got to find that wormhole to escape back to Annutia," she said with complete seriousness.

"Add to this the fact that algae blooms can grow massively within days or even hours," continued Connor calmly. "Imagine if all the algae blooms of the world experience explosive growth at the same time. They would suddenly link up through the waterways. Maybe this is how Annutia found itself so abruptly in an unforeseen crisis."

"You're right, Connor," agreed Lenore. "The algae blooms could have just exploded without warning and, in an instant, Annutians were fighting to survive. It sounds like we have enough algae on Earth that it could happen to us at any time. Suddenly humanity could be dying of algae toxicity – our water, our food chain, and the air we breathe poisoned."

Connor looked pensive. "I wonder if the Annutians ignored all these warning signs for decades in the same way we have on Earth?"

"No," said Lenore. "Algae were unknown to Annutia. But I bet that's what happened on Miasma."

"I think you're right," agreed Connor. What if Earth was the second off-world colonization terraformed but the terraformers inadvertently included algae in the mix. Therefore, they couldn't save their population by escaping to Earth as their off-world colony.

"They therefore had to terraform a new planet. Annutia. This time, they made certain they didn't include the algae. But maybe the algae traveled along the wormhole by accident.

"Maybe when the Annutians were bringing people or artifacts from Earth in the bubbles. They wouldn't have known that they needed to protect themselves."

"It may be worse than simply the spread of algae," interrupted Daniel. "Dead zones are also spreading." He began reading another article excerpt. 'Dead zones – areas of water so starved of oxygen that most marine life cannot survive there – are spreading.'"

"Yes," Connor said. Apparently, when the algae die, they decompose, sucking up oxygen as they sink to the bottom of waterways. Hypoxia and anoxia (the complete absence of dissolved oxygen) kill the aquatic organisms necessary to the food chain."

Daniel continued reading the article aloud. "'At the last count, there were 405 such zones worldwide, covering 245,000 square kilometers (94,600 square miles) – or an area slightly larger than the United Kingdom. In summer 2017, a dead zone in the Gulf of Mexico is set to approach more than 20,700 square kilometers – the largest expanse ever recorded there.'"[11]

"Listen to this headline," exclaimed movie-lover Connor. "'*Did a Deadly Algal Toxin Inspire Hitchcock's The Birds?*'"[12]

"That was a scary movie," exclaimed Lenore with a shudder. "Algae caused that?"

"It says, 'Famed horror movie director Alfred Hitchcock may have found inspiration for the 1963 film, *The Birds*, from a mass bird casualty that occurred near his home on August 18, 1961,'" read Connor. "'That morning, the residents of Capitola, California, awoke to the sight of hundreds of dead sooty shearwaters strewn across the streets and the sound of others ramming themselves into their roofs.

"'A mystery at the time it happened, scientists now believe the cause for this bizarre display of behavior was domoic acid, a deadly toxin released by algae exposed to urea pollution, reports *Nature's* Amy Coombs. Domoic acid is a toxin that causes extensive brain damage and provokes unusual behavior patterns that resemble homicidal tendencies – hence the large number of birds slamming into the residents' rooftops.

"'Over the last few decades, domoic acid has been responsible for several large outbreaks of deaths and illness. In 1998, 400 disoriented sea lions died along California's central coast – domoic acid was traced back to contaminated fish that swam through a toxic bloom before being eaten by the sea lions.'"

"This would mean that algae toxicity has been known at least from the early 60s," calculated an alarmed Daniel. "What have we been doing to stop the phosphorous-laden fertilizers and wastewater that has been feeding them?"

"Why hasn't the world done something? queried Lenore. Miasma and Annutia are cautionary tales. Unfortunately, we can't share them with the world to shake people awake."

"We have our work cut out for us," assessed Daniel. "We could sure use Mikael, Dania and the Berghs here now."

Connor suddenly smiled like a kid with a new toy. "I feel a new company coming on," he proclaimed with exhilaration. "The world is increasingly going to need creatives to solve life-threatening crises just as the Annutians did. We three are *a creatives factory*.

"We can move from issue to issue and cultivate those capable of inventing the solutions in a few months just as we did on Annutia. Dealing with Annutia's algae crisis is just a model we've proven will work. Our future isn't in algae specifically. *It's in releasing human potential, creativity, and invention to solve world crises.* This is our lane. Our jam.

"We've proven that we're great at selecting the right people to become creatives for a specific crisis and arming them with savanting methods for harnessing and exploiting the bioflow.

"If we move from crisis to crisis, eventually, we'll have seeded the planet with a creative force and the means to solve every problem that comes up quickly.

Our mission is to raise the adaptivity of humanity for survival.

"Personal and cultural changes can accomplish this faster than biological evolution. Our previous work released people to the application of their strongest talent. This next iteration will harvest creativity from one's greatest talents.

And we have a million dollars from Axl to get us started!"

"We do?" asked Daniel and Lenore together.

"Yes, I sold them the Annutian publishing rights for my book," said Connor.

"You finished *Savanting*?"

"I did."

"Did you bring it with you?"

"I did."

"Where is it? Where is the money?" asked Lenore.

"In this bag on the floor. Daniel could see the bag but Lenore had to roll over Connor to see it without getting out of bed.

"We're rich," cried Lenore with eyes as big as saucers.

"Are you suggesting that some of that money is mine?" asked Daniel. Am I now finally rich?"

"Could we get back to my idea?" complained Connor with a feigned impatience at Daniel's teasing. "You spoiled trust-fund brat."

"You're talking shades of the old Chinese Proverb," said Lenore. 'Give a man a fish and you feed him for a day. Teach a man to fish and you feed him for a lifetime.'"

"Right," agreed Connor. "And look what we did in a few months on Annutia. All our creatives fished exceedingly well and will continue to do so for the rest of their lives."

"It's so unfortunate that we can't use them as a reference," laughed Daniel.

"I dare you to try to explain our Annutia credentials to a potential client," teased Lenore. They all laughed. "I think we best make a pact not to tell anyone. Our professional reputations will be destroyed. Who would believe us anyway?

"The important thing is that *we* know what we can do and how fast we can do it with minimal resources and planning. We never would have known we weren't operating at our maximum without the Annutia experience pushing us to our limits."

"All we need do is be true to our talents, strengths, passions, and the bioflow," prescribed Connor. "We aren't algae experts. After all, the bioflow already orchestrated a more incredible encore than any of us could have foreseen or asked to have. Why would we doubt it will do it again?

"You're right," agreed Daniel. "The bioflow may prioritize other crises higher than the pending algae crisis to benefit all living systems on Earth. Some other crisis may stretch us to even greater maximums. We simply need to be open to its direction. Annutia could be just the model provided by the bioflow to show us our path out of our post-retirement void.

To keep us in serial savantflows at our maximum, we must be stretched beyond our previous capabilities," said Lenore thinking out loud. The bioflow will therefore be orchestrating contexts which demand that we operate at new levels of maximization. That's all we can know at this point.

"But, wouldn't it be amazing if Annutia was a trial run for saving Earth from a worldwide algae plague?" exclaimed Connor excitedly. "Absolutely the entire pattern of events – these most incredible miraculous events – over the last few months demonstrates that the bioflow is pulling us in this direction. Everything we've read here today has also carried us in this direction. Lenore, remember the last time we saw a pattern this strong?"

"When we formulated the upgrade of the world's human resources to full potential to address the crises ten years ago," responded Lenore.

"I think this constellation of coincidences, breakthroughs, and facilitating events is exponentially stronger and more profound?"

"I agree in spades, Connor," said Lenore. "You're totally right. How amazing of the universal bioflow maximizing machinery to have accomplished this to save Earth and humanity."

"In addition to the plethora of patterns, my resonance is also strong," said Connor. "It's saying 'Yes' to the prospect of repeating what we did on Annutia to save Earth."

"My resonance says 'Yes' too!" exclaimed Lenore with great enthusiasm. "Doing it faster and better than before for the world we love."

"My resonance agrees!" said Daniel emphatically.

Everyone smiled at each other with the prospect of their next big adventure.

"'It's déjà vu all over again,'" laughed Connor. Only an imperfect Yogi-ism from American baseball great Yogi Berra could so perfectly capture this perfect encore.

THE END

---

[1] *Toxic algae: Once a nuisance, now a severe nationwide threat* by John Flesher and Angeliki Kastanis, 11-16-2017, retrieved from https://www.apnews.com/8ca7048f5cff4b45a634296a358f7309

[2] *Toxic algae becoming severe threat nationwide* by Paul Sancya, 11-16-2017, retrieved from https://www.cbsnews.com/news/toxic-algae-severe-threat-nationwide/

[3] *It's not just Ohio—poisonous algae blooms now plague 20 US states* by Gwynn Guilford, 8-4-2014, retrieved from https://qz.com/244387/poisonous-algae-blooms-now-plague-20-states-around-the-us-not-just-ohio/

[4] *Lake Erie algae bloom grew so large, it broke the scale* by Scott Sutherland, 11-23-2015, retrieved from https://www.theweathernetwork.com/news/articles/lake-erie-toxic-algae-spreads-to-largest-extent-on-record/60182

[5] *Toxic algae: Once a nuisance, now a severe nationwide threat* by John Flesher and Angeliki Kastanis, 11-16-2017, retrieved from https://www.apnews.com/8ca7048f5cff4b45a634296a358f7309

[6] *Toxic Algae Blooms Occurring More Often, May Be Caught in Climate Change Feedback Loop* by Georgina Gustin, 5-15-2018, retrieved from https://insideclimatenews.org/news/15052018/algae-blooms-climate-change-methane-emissions-data-agriculture-nutrient-runoff-fertilizer-sewage-pollution-lake-erie

[7] *Harmful Algal Bloom*, Wikipedia, retrieved from https://en.wikipedia.org/wiki/Harmful_algal_bloom

[8] *Massive Algae Bloom Spreading Across Baltic Sea* by Jennifer Hattam, 7-24-2010, retrieved from https://www.treehugger.com/natural-sciences/massive-algae-bloom-spreading-across-baltic-sea.html

[9] *Toxic seaweed on French coast sparks health fears* by Henry Samuel, Paris, 7-22-2011, retrieved from https://www.telegraph.co.uk/news/worldnews/europe/france/8655329/Toxic-seaweed-on-French-coast-sparks-health-fears.html

[10] *Killer Algae Migrates to California Coast / Mediterranean species found near San Diego* by David Perlman, Chronicle Science Editor, 7-6-2000, retrieved from https://www.sfgate.com/science/article/Killer-Algae-Migrates-to-California-Coast-3238615.php

[11] *Ocean 'dead zones' cover an area larger than the United Kingdom* by Jennifer Collins, 03-08-2017, retrieved from https://www.dw.com/en/ocean-dead-zones-cover-an-area-larger-than-the-united-kingdom/a-39941558

[12] *Did a Deadly Algal Toxin Inspire Hitchcock's 'The Birds'* by Jeremy Elton Jacquot, 10-29-2008, retrieved from https://www.treehugger.com/corporate-responsibility/did-a-deadly-algal-toxin-inspire-hitchcocks-the-birds.html

ABOUT THE AUTHOR

Lauren Holmes is the CEO of Frontiering which maximizes talent and creates worldbuilders using her *savanting* achievement technology introduced in *The Encore: A Transformational Thriller* and her upcoming book, *Savanting.* An early iteration was captured in her 2001 bestseller, *Peak Evolution: Beyond Peak Performance and Peak Experience.*

Lauren's education and career were designed to allow her to develop and test every part of *savanting*: She has a biological anthropology degree from the University of Toronto. After first becoming a change leader in global banks, she launched an executive search firm for change leaders for the boards and C-suites of large multinationals. This evolved into providing executive change leaders on contract before that field existed.

Recruiting executives evolved into executive coaching before that field existed. Coaching matured into co-creating new ventures and frontiers customized to ensure client success. This unprecedented field capitalizes on Lauren's gift as an execution creative as described in *The Encore*.

Lauren Holmes now provides talent maximization, execution leadership, and the invention of customized new frontiers for aspiring worldbuilders. She is also planning a movie script for *The Encore.*